Uncle Robert's Geography

This edition published 2025
by Living Book Press
Copyright © Living Book Press, 2025

ISBN: 978-1-76153-281-8 (hardcover)
         978-1-76153-282-5 (softcover)

First published in 1904.

A catalogue record for this book is available from the National Library of Australia

Uncle Robert's Geography

by

Francis W. Parker

LIVING BOOK
PRESS

THE FARMHOUSE.

Contents

AUTHOR'S PREFACE

Fortunate are the children whose early years are spent in the country in close contact with the boundless riches which Nature bestows.

Amid these environments instinct and spontaneity do a marvelous work in the growing minds of children, arousing and sustaining varied and various interests, enhancing mental activities, and furnishing an educative outlet for lively energies.

Most fortunate are they to whom, at the moment when the unconscious teachings of Nature need to be supplemented by thoughtful suggestion, wise leadings, and judicious instruction, there comes one with a deep and loving sympathy with child life, an active interest in all that interests them, and a profound respect for all that children do well and for all that they know.

Such an one is Uncle Robert. He comes to the children at just the right moment. He directs the sweet strong streams of their lives onward into a channel of earnest inquiry and exalted labor, which is ever broadening and deepening.

Uncle Robert's aim in education is to fill each day with acts which make home better, the community better, mankind better; to take from God's bounteous and boundless store of truth and convert it into human life by using it. His method is simple and direct, founded upon the firm rock, Common Sense. It may be briefly stated as follows:

1. A strong belief in the sacredness of work—that work which inspires thought, strengthens the body as well as the mind, and develops the feeling of usefulness.

2. The images the children have acquired and the inferences they have made are used as stepping stones to higher and broader views.

3. So far as it is possible, each child is to discover facts for himself and make original inferences.

4. He understands the limits of children's power to observe and the demand on their part for glimpses into, to them, the great unknown. So he tells them stories of those things which lie beyond

their horizon, in order to excite their wonder, intensify their love for the objects that surround them, and make them more careful observers. In this way a hunger and thirst for books is created.

5. He watches carefully the interests of each child, adapting his teachings to the differences in age and personality.

6. Some questions are left unanswered in order to stimulate that healthy curiosity which can be satisfied only by persistent study—the study that begets courage and confidence.

7. He makes farm work and farm life full of intensely interesting problems, ever keeping in mind that the things of which the common environments of common lives are made up are as well worthy of study as are those which lie beyond.

Uncle Robert's enthusiasm has for its prime impulse a boundless faith in human progress, brought about by a knowledge of childhood and its possibilities.

He believes that every normal child, under wise and loving guidance, may become useful to his fellows, moral in character, strong in intellect, with a body which is an efficient instrument of the soul; in other words, truly educated.

Those who read Uncle Robert's Visit should read through the eyes of Susie, Donald, and Frank. The reading, so far as possible, should be accompanied by personal observation, investigation, and experiment.

FRANCIS W. PARKER.
CHICAGO NORMAL SCHOOL,
August 31, 1897.

TOPICAL ANALYSIS OF UNCLE ROBERT'S VISIT.

NOTE.—The direct study of earth, air, and water involves the study of plant, animal, and human life. Popular opinion has given the name of geography to these correlated subjects.

CHAPTER I.—UNCLE ROBERT'S COMING.

The value of the children's knowledge of the farm is warmly recognized by Uncle Robert. The children feel his sympathy for their work, and through it are led to closer study and investigation. The feeling that everything they may see and do is of importance, exalts their daily life.

Encourage children to describe the farms on which they live. In such descriptions should come plant and animal life, and the means and processes of farm work. Extend these descriptions to other farms and to any landscapes which the children have observed.

CHAPTER II.—FRANK DRAWS A MAP OF THE FARM.

All children love to draw, and they will draw with great confidence and boldness unless their critical faculty outruns their skill. Modeling and painting may be very profitably introduced at an early age. Frank's efforts in drawing strengthened his images of the landscape.

Arithmetic has a very important place in farm life. It may be used in many ways in forming habits of accuracy and exactness.

CHAPTER III.—THE NEW THERMOMETER.

The children have their first lesson on the agent of all physical movement and change in organic and inorganic matter. The simple experiments suggested should be continued and enlarged, thus beginning a life study of a subject which is practically unlimited in its importance to man.

CHAPTER IV.—WITH THE ANIMALS.

Children look upon animals as their particular friends and acquaintances. They talk to them and believe that the animals understand them. A desire to know the habits and habitats of animals is among their strongest interests. By a little wise direction, this interest may be so enhanced as to form a substantial beginning of the study of zoology.

CHAPTER V.—IN THE FLOWER GARDEN.

Children worship flowers. Probably there are no objects on earth so universally loved by little folks as buds and flowers. Children seek eagerly for flowers by the roadside, in the pastures, fields, and woods. This love, like all instincts, should be carefully cultivated.

Children may easily be led to study the forms, colors, and habits of plants. They will always take the keenest interest in the mystery of seeds and shoots, of roots and growing leaves, *if there is a teacher to direct them.*

CHAPTER VI.—SUNLIGHT AND SHADOW.

We have heat again, and now as an elementary lesson in the distribution of sunshine. Children love to observe continual changes. The shadow is an object of interest. It has an element of mystery about it which borders upon the supernatural.

Children observe spontaneously the long shadows of morning and the lengthening shadows of the descending sun. Most farm boys can tell the moment of noon by their shadows.

These are all steps in the more difficult problems of lengthening and shortening shadows that mark the changing seasons, and that lead to the theories of the earth's rotation and revolution. Day by day children should note the changes of slant upon the shadow stick which they can easily make for themselves.

CHAPTER VII.—THE BAROMETER.

Our little friends have their first lesson concerning one of the three great envelopes of the earth—the atmosphere. The knowledge that air has weight does not often come by unaided intuition. The initial experiments may be made very interesting and profitable. The United States Weather Reports are an excellent means for the home study of geography.

CHAPTER VIII.—A WALK IN THE WOODS.

"There is pleasure in the pathless woods" and "The groves were God's first temples" are lines which appeal strongly to those who have spent hours in the shadows and flickering sunlight of the forest. Trees well arranged make many farmhouses beautiful. Trees by the roadside add much beauty to the landscape and afford places of rest to the traveler.

Forests mean moisture to the soil. Their leaves and roots make the best reservoirs for water, to be given out when needed by the growing crops. The forests are full of lessons for the children and the experienced scientist.

CHAPTER IX.—THE BIRDS AND THE FLOWERS.

The knowledge of a farm child is quite extensive, and generally neither the child nor the parent has any suspicion that such knowledge is of any appreciable value in education. It is clearly within the bounds of possibility for every farm boy and girl to know every bird that lives on the farm in summer or winter, and those who rest there in their migrating flight; to know also the names, the plumage, the habits of all the birds; and to know the nests and nesting places of those who make the farm their summer home.

All this study cultivates the child's sense of the beautiful. There is no better color study in the world than that which springs from discriminating love of flowers and of the plumage of birds. Such study creates a kindly feeling toward both animals and plants on the part of the child. It exercises a strong moral power over him.

CHAPTER X.—THE THUNDERSHOWER.

A thundershower is always a phenomenon of interest and often of fear on the part of children. The clouds of the cumulus form, the rolling of thunder, the lightning flashes, the rushing wind, and the pouring rain are full of important lessons. Fear vanishes as knowledge comes. In the thundershower is the question of the distribution of moisture over the earth's surface, the question of the nature and use of clouds, the movement of the air and wind, the condensation of vapor, and the marvelous powers of electricity.

CHAPTER XI.—THE VILLAGE.

Geography should ever be in the closest touch with the human side. Nature does a marvelous work, but Nature without society is like a vast storehouse of treasure without a demand for its use. The one weak point in farm life is the lack of opportunity for contact with society.

CHAPTER XII.—A DAY ON THE RIVER.

A river, creek, lake—in fact, any body of water—is a source of perpetual delight to children. Frank, Donald, and Susie have had the river and creek before them all their lives. Now, under Uncle Robert's teaching, the river will mean very much more to them. They take their first lessons in the work of streams in carving and shaping the earth's surface. The pebbles on the beach and the large, rounded stones will soon have stories of the distant past to tell them. The "Big Book" is opened to them, and they read the stories directly from its pages.

CHAPTER XIII.—A RAINY DAY.

The children get closer to the question of moisture, its use, and distribution. The rain gauge helps them to measure the rainfall. Then comes the problem of where the water goes after it reaches the ground. "How far down does some of it go?" "When and where does it come out of the ground?"

Arithmetic is brought in in measuring the rainfall and its distribution.

CHAPTER XIV.—THE WALK AFTER THE RAIN.

The problems in Chapter XIII move toward their solution, and new questions are opened. The gully tells of the wearing of the water, and foretells a river valley. The spring helps in the question of underground water. The flowing river quickens the imagination in the direction of the great ocean.

CHAPTER XV.—THE BIG BOOK.

This chapter should be read by parents to the children, as many sentences need expansion and explanation. Hints are given of great things which lie beyond the child's horizon. Discoveries that have changed mankind are referred to.

Children's permanent interests are the keynotes of instruction and the infallible guides of the teacher. To continue and sustain their spontaneous observation and desire for investigation leads directly to the study of the best books, and lays the basis for a thorough and profound study of God's universe.

CHAPTER I.

UNCLE ROBERT'S COMING.

Uncle Robert was coming. His letter, telling when they should expect him, had been received a week before. Every day since had been full of talks and plans for his visit, and now the day was come. Everything was ready.

Frank and Donald had harnessed Nell, the old white horse, to the little spring wagon, and had driven to the village to meet the train which was to bring Uncle Robert from New York.

Susie, in her prettiest white apron, ran out of the house every few minutes, to be the first to see them when they should come along the road.

Mrs. Leonard was putting finishing touches here and there. She went into the kitchen to give Jane a last direction about the supper. Then she went to the east room upstairs, Uncle Robert's room, to be sure that everything was just as she knew he would like it.

Susie followed her mother, to see if the violets in the glass on his table were still bright and fresh. She had gathered them herself in the woods that morning.

"There they come!" she cried. "I hear the wagon crossing the bridge at the creek!"

She ran quickly downstairs and out upon the piazza. A moment more, and the wagon turned in at the gate.

9

"Mother, mother," called Susie, "they're here!"

But Mrs. Leonard was already beside her. Her pleasant face glowed with a happy smile as Frank drew rein before the door.

Then such a time!

Uncle Robert sprang from the seat beside Frank, hugged Mrs. Leonard, then Susie, then both together.

Donald, who was seated in the back of the wagon on Uncle Robert's trunk, turned a handspring, landed on his feet somehow or other, and stood grinning at Susie.

Mr. Leonard had also heard the sound of the wheels. He hurried from the barn, calling Peter to come and help him carry Uncle Robert's trunk upstairs.

Jane came to the door of the dining-room, eager to see the Uncle Robert of whom she had heard so much. Then, with a nod of her head, she ran back, slipped the pan of biscuits into the oven, and put the kettle on to boil.

Uncle Robert had come! Everybody was happy. No one more so than Uncle Robert himself.

"Now, this is good," he said, when at length they were seated around the supper table. "I feel at home already. Susie, did those violets on my table grow in your garden?"

"Oh, no," replied Susie. "I found them in the woods by the creek. And the buttercups, didn't you see them in the glass, too?"

VIOLETS.

"Buttercups so early?" asked Uncle Robert. "Oh, yes, the low ones do come early. You must take me down where they grow some day."

"We'll go to-morrow," said Susie.

Uncle Robert smiled at the eager little face, and, turning to Mr. Leonard, said:

"Frank tells me the farm is looking well this spring."

"Yes, it looks fairly well," replied Mr. Leonard. "The seed is all in but the corn. That is a little late. The water on the bottom land stayed longer than usual this year."

"Peter thinks we can start the planting to-morrow," said Frank.

"Yes," replied his father, "I think so, too."

When supper was over they all went out on the side porch. The sun was setting. The air was soft and spring-like. The lilacs along the fence filled the air with fragrance.

"Don't you want to see Susie's garden, Robert?" asked Mrs. Leonard,

"Yes, indeed," said Uncle Robert. "Susie wrote me some nice little letters about that garden."

As they walked along the narrow paths Susie showed him where the seeds were already planted, and told him what she thought she would have in the other beds.

"This is phlox," said Susie, leading Uncle Robert by the hand; "and marigolds are here, and sweet peas over there by the fence. That place between mother's garden and mine is filled with rosebushes, syringas, and hollyhocks."

"I still call the vegetable garden mine, but the boys do most of the work," said Mrs. Leonard. "That big bush at the end of the row is an elder."

"This is to be my pansy bed," said Susie. "The pansies are

PANSIES.

not set out yet. They are growing in a box in the kitchen window. I love them best of all. Don't they look like funny little faces in bonnets?"

"That is what the Germans think, Susie," said Uncle Robert, laughing. "They call them 'little stepmothers.'"

"I think it will be safe to put them out soon, Susie," said Mrs. Leonard.

"Mother," called Donald from the vegetable garden, "the lettuce and radishes are growing finely, and here's a bean. Oh, there are lots of them just putting their heads through!"

They all went over to look at the beans, and then walked down to the end of the garden where the currant and gooseberry bushes grew.

"Oh, uncle," exclaimed Susie, "I wish you had come in time to see the trees in blossom! They were all pink and white. It was just lovely! only the flowers stayed such a little while."

"I think Susie lived in the orchard those days," said Mrs. Leonard, smiling. "If I wanted her I was very sure to find her there."

APPLE BLOSSOMS.

"I don't blame Susie," said Uncle Robert. "I would have stayed, too. There is nothing sweeter than apple blossoms. But you have other fruits besides apples, haven't you?"

"Oh, yes," said Frank, who had just come from the barn, where he had gone after supper with his father. "There are pears and cherries and a few peach trees. But peaches don't do well here."

"The blossoms are lovely," said Susie.

"I believe Susie cares more for the flowers than she does for the fruit," said Donald. "I don't. I like the fruit, and plenty of it."

"How many kinds of apples have you?" asked Uncle Robert.

"About ten," replied Frank. "But father budded quite a number last year. The twigs came from Kansas."

"They have fine apples in Kansas some years," said Uncle Robert. "I wonder if the budding is done as it was when I was a boy on the farm in New England."

"This is the way father did it," said Frank. "First he cut a little piece of the bark off the twig with the bud on it. He had to do it very carefully with a sharp knife. Then he cut the bark on the branch of the tree like the letter T. He laid it back, and slipped the piece of bark with the bud on under it. Then he bound it all up with soft cotton, and left it to take care of itself."

"Did it?" asked Uncle Robert.

"Yes," answered Donald. "In a few weeks we took the binding off, and the bark had all grown together around the little bud."

"There were ever so many of them," said Susie, "and they were all alike."

"I wish they would hurry up and have

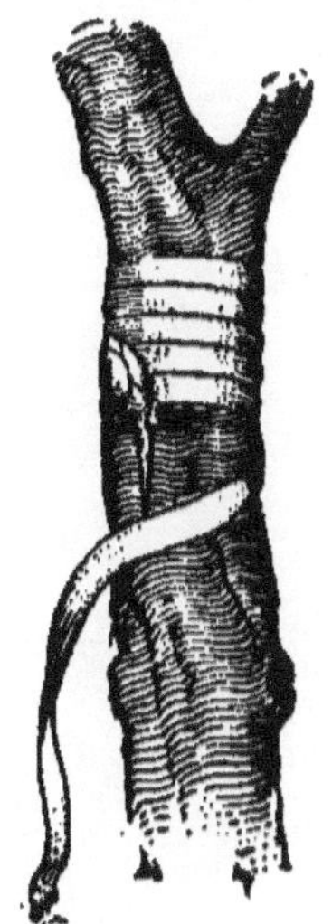

BUDDING

some apples on them," said Donald. "If they're better than some we had last year, they'll be pretty good.

"Come, children," said Mrs. Leonard. "It is getting damp. I think we'd better go in now."

CHAPTER II

FRANK DRAWS A MAP OF THE FARM.

After the lamps were lighted and they were all gathered in the sitting-room Uncle Robert began asking the children about the farm.

"What do you raise besides corn?" he asked.

"Wheat, oats, rye, and potatoes," said Frank. "Then we have the hay fields and the pasture. The woods we drove through coming from town belong to us too."

"The house faces east, doesn't it?" said Uncle Robert. "That would make the woods north. Where are all these other fields?"

"Back of the barn and the other side of the orchard," said Donald.

"Can't some one show me on paper how it is?" asked Uncle Robert. "I don't mean make a picture, but just a plan of it."

"Well, I can try," said Frank. "I know just how it is really, but I don't know that I can get it right."

Frank found paper and pencil and set to work, while the rest gathered eagerly around and looked on.

"This is the river," he said. "There's a big curve in it along our farm. The road runs along the top of the slope, and this is where the house is."

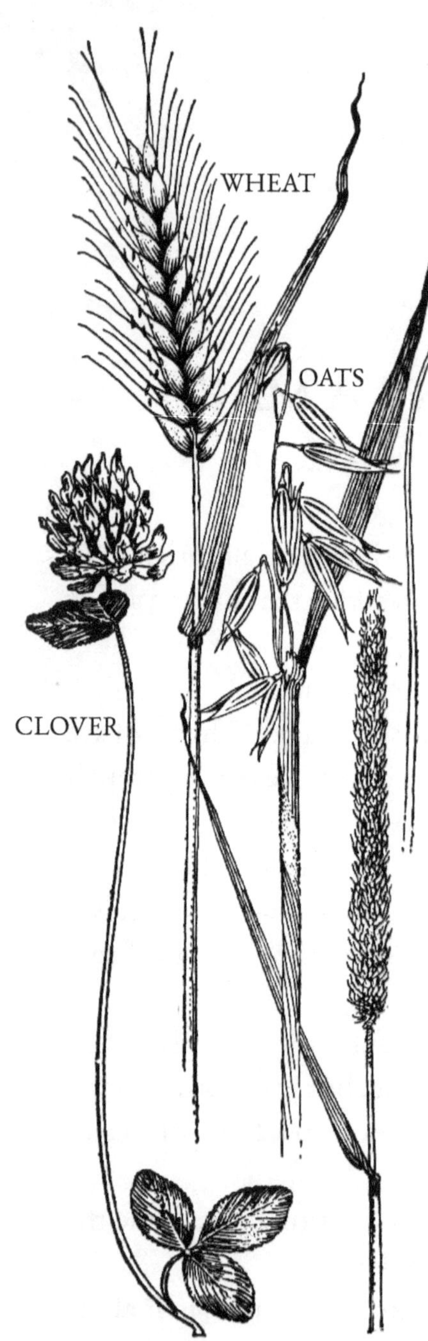

"What lies between the house and the river?" asked Uncle Robert.

"The big cornfield," said Frank. "That's where we are going to plant to-morrow if it is a pleasant day. And right here, in the corner by the woods, is the spring."

"The water comes right out of the ground," said Susie; "and it is as cold as ice."

"Here," said Frank, "is the wood. You know we drove through it this afternoon. The woods are on both sides of the creek."

"See the crooked line he makes for the creek," said Donald.

"That is where the violets and buttercups grow, uncle," said Susie, pointing to the map.

"Where does the creek come from?" asked Uncle Robert.

"There's a pond away back

in the woods," said Donald. "It comes from that; but it is a swamp part of the year."

"The cat-tails grow there," said Susie.

"Well," said Uncle Robert, "the house, the cornfield, and the woods—is that all of the farm?"

"Oh, no!" said Frank. "It is low along the river, but back of the cornfield it gets higher, and that's where the grapes are. On this side of the road is the orchard; and here, between the orchard and the woods, come in the yard and garden."

"Don't leave out the barnyard," said Donald.

"What's back of the barn?" asked Uncle Robert.

"The field of timothy; and next to it is the clover field. That is as far as the farm goes that way."

"The wheat field is on the other side of the timothy, Frank," said Donald, "and the oats between that and the road, beside the orchard."

"Put in the potatoes along the road," said Susie.

"Now all we have left is the rye field over in the corner," said Donald.

"That is the way it is this year," said Mr. Leonard, who sat with his paper in his hand. But the paper was unread. He found the group around the table much more interesting.

"Now it is all done," said Susie, hopping about on one foot. "Isn't it fun? Let's draw the garden. I can do it."

"All right," said Uncle Robert, "you shall; but I think we'd better finish the farm first. Who can tell how many acres there are in each of these lots?"

"I know there are twenty in the timothy meadow," said Donald, "because father always calls it the twenty-acre lot."

"Write it down on the map, Frank," said Uncle Robert. "How much in the clover field?"

"It seems about half as large as the timothy meadow," said Frank.

"That's right," said Mr. Leonard; "it is."

"There are twenty acres in the wood lot, aren't there, father?" asked Frank. "It isn't quite so wide, but it is longer than the timothy meadow."

"Yes," said Mr. Leonard, "there are twenty acres there; and it is as fine woodland as any I know."

"There are ten acres in the orchard," said Frank; "and the cornfield is the largest of all."

"That must be thirty acres," said Donald. "I remember when father made the pasture smaller, so that we could have more corn."

"Yes," said Frank; "and that left ten in the pasture. I remember. And there are fifteen acres each in oats, wheat, and rye; but I don't know how large the potato field is. It is smaller than the others, though—it must be about ten."

"Right again," said Mr. Leonard.

"Now we have it all but the yard and garden," said Uncle Robert. "Does any one know how much land they cover?"

The father and mother looked on smiling, but said nothing.

$$
\begin{array}{r}
20 \\
10 \\
20 \\
10 \\
30 \\
10 \\
15 \\
15 \\
15 \\
10 \\
\hline
165
\end{array}
\qquad
\begin{array}{r}
160 \\
165 \\
\hline
5
\end{array}
$$

"It's all the rest of the farm, anyhow," said Susie.

"Oh, I know how to find out," said Frank. "We know the whole farm is one hundred and sixty acres. We can add all these figures, and the difference between that and one hundred and sixty will be what's in the yard and garden."

So he added all the numbers together and found them to be one hundred and fifty-five.

"Yes," exclaimed Donald; "and five more would make it one hundred and sixty."

"Then there must be five acres in the yard and garden." said Susie, "Write it down. Frank."

"There," said Frank, looking at his work with some pride. "It's all in. Now shall I draw it again and make the lines straighter?"

"Oh, no; this tells the story very well," said Uncle Robert. "The next time we will measure it off, and make it more carefully."

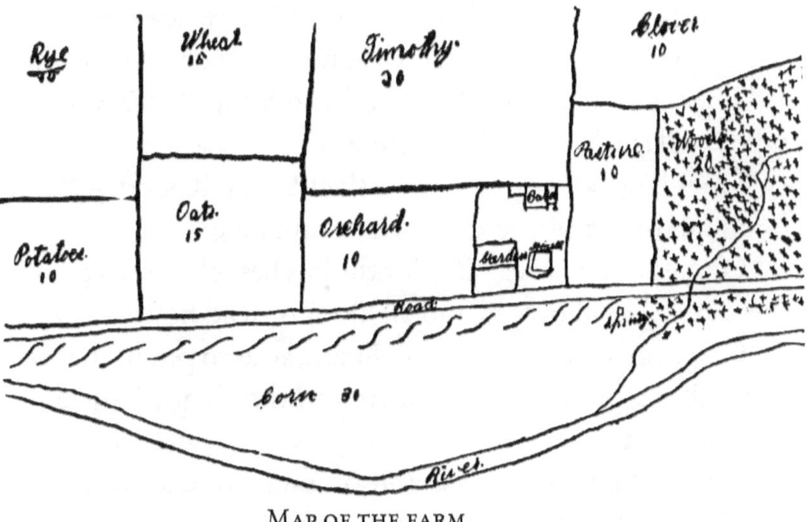

MAP OF THE FARM.

"Not so bad," said Mr. Leonard, as Frank showed him the drawing.

"I think it is very good for a first time," said Mrs. Leonard, with an encouraging smile. "With a little practice, my boy, I believe you would draw well."

"Mother always believes we can do things," said Frank, laughing.

"Tell me more about the river," said Uncle Robert.

"Our side is bottom land," said Frank; "but across the river the bank is high and steep. Farther down it is just the other way. The steep bank is on this side, and the low land is opposite."

"The river bends the other way down there," said Donald.

"I see," said Uncle Robert. "How high is the bank?"

"I don't know," answered Frank. "How high is it, father?"

"About twenty feet," said Mr. Leonard.

"Do you go on the river much?" asked Uncle Robert.

"Oh, yes," said Donald. "We have an old boat, and we have been miles on it."

"That is, downstream," said Frank. "We have never taken the boat up the river beyond the village, on account of the milldam."

"There's an island in the river," said Susie, "between here and the village. We have been there."

"How large an island is it?" asked Uncle Robert—"large enough to have a picnic there while I am here?"

"Oh, yes," said Susie. "It's just the loveliest place for a picnic! There are trees all over it, and all kinds of wild flowers."

"Can't you extend your map, Frank, so as to put in the river to the village, showing the milldam and the island?" suggested Uncle Robert.

"You might draw it this way, too," said Donald, "and show how the river bends the other way down here."

"Now I want to draw my garden," said Susie, when Frank had finished.

Just then the clock on the kitchen shelf struck loudly.

"It's bedtime now, dear," said Mrs. Leonard. "Can't you draw your garden to-morrow?"

"We'll plant those pansies to-morrow," said Uncle Robert, "and see what can be put in all the other beds. Then we'll draw it, and tell just where everything is."

So Susie went to bed happy, and Frank and Donald soon followed. And all were glad that Uncle Robert was really come.

CHAPTER III

THE NEW THERMOMETER.

The next morning as they left the breakfast table Donald said:

"It's going to be warmer to-day."

"I think not," said Frank. "When I went to the barn it seemed quite cool."

"What do you think, Susie?" asked Uncle Robert.

"It was cool under the trees when I went to the spring for a pitcher of water," said Susie, "but it seemed rather warm in the sun. I think it is a lovely morning."

"What makes it warm?" asked Uncle Robert.

"Why, the sun," replied Donald, looking rather surprised at such a question.

"But does the sun make it warm in the winter?" asked Uncle Robert.

"The sun is nearer the earth in spring and summer," said Frank confidently.

"You are mistaken," said Uncle Robert. "The sun is farther from us in summer than it is in winter."

"But it's almost over our heads in summer," said Frank. "How can it be farther away?"

"The story of the warmth that the sun gives us is not told by distance," said Uncle Robert, "but by the length of the shadows at noon."

"How is that?" asked Donald.

"When is your shadow the longest?" asked Uncle Robert.

"In the evening," said Donald.

"In the morning," said Susie.

"When is your shadow the shortest?"

"At noon!" they all shouted.

"When is it coolest?"

"Morning," they replied together.

"When is it warmest?"

"Noon," said Susie quickly.

"Now you are wrong," said Frank. "It is often warmer at one or two o'clock."

"Frank is right," said Uncle Robert. "How can we tell just how warm it is at any time?"

"If we had a thermometer," said Donald, "that would tell, but we haven't."

"There's one at the post office," said Frank, "but I never saw any one look at it unless it was very cold or very hot."

"Perhaps we can find one nearer than the post office," said Uncle Robert. "Susie, would you know one if you saw it?"

Susie shook her head.

"I would," said Donald.

"Well," said Uncle Robert, "please go to my room, and if you find a thermometer bring it to me."

Donald soon returned, and when Susie saw what he had in his hand she exclaimed:

"Is that a thermometer? I never saw anything like that at the post office."

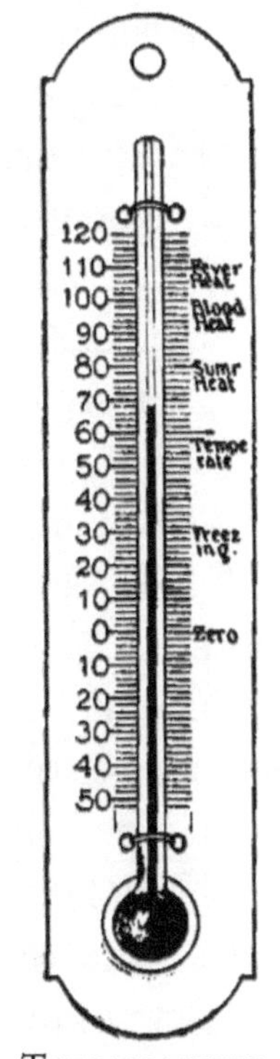

THERMOMETER.

"Well, I should think not," said Donald. "This isn't much like the old thing they have up there."

"What does it say?" asked Uncle Robert.

"Sixty-eight degrees above zero," said Frank, taking the thermometer in his hand.

"That isn't cold, is it, uncle?" asked Donald.

"That's just right for the house," said Uncle Robert. "How is it out of doors?"

"Let's take it out and see," said Frank.

Out on the porch they went and eagerly watched the thermometer.

"It's moving—it's going down!" cried Donald.

"I'll hang it on this nail," said Frank.

"When they looked again Donald said:

"It's fifty-six now."

"How much colder is it than it was in the house?" asked Uncle Robert.

"Twelve degrees," said Frank, counting up the column.

"Oh, let's take it in by the stove," said Susie, "and see how far it will go up."

"What makes you think it will go up by the stove?" asked Uncle Robert.

"Well," answered Susie, "if it goes down when it is cold I should think it would go up when it is warm."

Susie took the little instrument, and, going into the kitchen, held it close to the stove.

"Come," she called, "it is going up already. See!"

"How fast it moves!" said Donald. "Hold it close to the stove, Susie. Maybe it will go to the very top."

"Let us put it in cold water," said Frank. "It won't hurt the thermometer, will it?"

"Not at all," was the reply. "Try it."

So they held it in the bucket of cold spring water.

"How fast it goes down now!" said Susie. "I wonder if it will go lower than it did out on the porch. It's down to forty-eight."

"Why does Jane set the kettle of cold water on the stove?" asked Uncle Robert, pointing to it.

"To boil the water," answered Susie.

"What makes the water boil?"

"Why, the fire, of course."

"How long will the stove stay hot?"

"As long as there is fire in it."

"Longer than that," said Donald. "It doesn't grow cold the minute the fire is out."

"What becomes of all the heat?" asked Uncle Robert.

"Oh, it goes all round the room."

"Let's put the thermometer in the hot water," said Susie.

"Oh, see it go up!" said Donald. "It is one hundred and fifteen already."

"What is the difference in degrees between the cold and the hot water?" asked Uncle Robert.

"Sixty-seven degrees," said Frank.

"What makes the difference in degrees?"

"The difference in the heat," said Frank.

"If the water was boiling and the thermometer large enough," said Uncle Robert, "it would go to two hundred and twelve."

"That would be ninety-seven degrees higher," said Frank.

"Wouldn't that be a big thermometer!" exclaimed Susie.

"Now put the thermometer on the floor," said Uncle Robert.

"It's seventy-two degrees now," said Donald in a few minutes.

"Let's put it on the broom," said Susie, "and hold it up to the ceiling."

"It's warmer up there," said Frank, looking at the little gray cylinder when they brought it down. "It is six degrees higher than it was on the floor."

"Why?" asked Uncle Robert.

"The heat must go up there," said Donald.

"It goes into the next room when the door is open," said Frank.

"Does it go outdoors?" asked Uncle Robert.

"Let's open the window and see," said Susie.

Frank opened the window, but, instead of feeling the warm air going out, he felt the cool air coming in.

"Uncle," asked Donald, "isn't the room full of air already?"

"Yes," answered Uncle Robert.

"Then I don't see how any more can come in at the window."

"Are you sure none goes out?"

"I could feel it coming in," said Frank.

"Jane," asked Uncle Robert, "have you a candle?"

"Here is one, sir," said Jane, taking a candlestick from beside the clock on the shelf.

Uncle Robert lighted it and held it near the window, just below the sill. The flame flickered as the air from the window struck it, and then turned straight into the room. He raised it just above the opening. Instantly the flame pointed toward the window, but it did not flicker as it had when held below the sill.

"The air must be going out up there," said Frank, "but it doesn't blow so strongly as the air coming in."

"The air that comes in is cooler than the air that goes out," said Donald.

"What makes the water boil?" asked Uncle Robert, turning to the kettle on the stove, which had now begun to sing.

"Why, the heat, of course," said Donald.

"What raises the lid?" asked Uncle Robert.

"The kettle is too full," said Frank. "It is going to boil over."

"Why didn't the water run over when it was cold?" asked Uncle Robert. "The kettle didn't seem full then."

"Somehow it seems to get more than full when it boils," said Donald. "See, it is boiling over."

Just then Jane took a pan of apples out of the oven. Each one looked like a small volcano.

"What happens to the apples when they bake?" asked Uncle Robert.

"They just swell up so big their jackets won't hold them," said Donald, laughing.

"It is heat that makes the bread rise, isn't it?" asked Frank.

"Of course," said Susie. "Don't you know sometimes if the bread doesn't rise, mother says it is because it is too cold?"

"There is something besides heat that makes the bread rise," said Uncle Robert.

"Yes," replied Susie, "the yeast; but it must be warm—I know it must."

"It seems as though everything is bigger when it is hot than when it is cold," said Frank. "And now I believe I understand something that happened not long ago."

"What was it?" asked Uncle Robert.

"Peter and I were driving to town," began Frank, "and the tire of one of the wagon wheels slipped right off. We managed to get to the blacksmith's shop, and he put the tire in the fire until it was hot. Then he put it on the wheel, but it was still loose. We couldn't have gone a step without its coming off again. He brought cold water and poured over it, and soon it was as tight as could be. I thought the water made the wood of the wheel swell up—you know water does that to the pails and tubs when they leak; but now I believe the fire made the

The blacksmith shop.

tire larger, and then the cold water made it small again. That is just what happened."

"But air can't grow bigger, can it?" asked Donald.

"If you can find an empty bottle, Donald," said Uncle Robert, "perhaps we can soon find out about it."

Uncle Robert took a piece of thin rubber out of his pocket and tied it tightly over the mouth of the bottle."

"By the way," he said, "is there anything in this bottle?

"No," said Susie, looking through the glass.

"Oh, yes," said Donald, "there is air in it."

"Well," replied Uncle Robert, "please get a pan of hot water, Frank."

Frank brought the water, and as Uncle Robert began to put the bottle into it they all exclaimed:

"Be careful; you'll break the bottle!"

"What will make it break?" asked Uncle Robert, pausing.

"Why, the hot water," said Susie.

"It always breaks glass if you put it in too quickly," said Donald.

"Well, we'll warm it a little first," holding the bottle close to the water. "I think I can try it now."

As he spoke he lowered the bottle into the water, and the rubber tied over the neck began to bulge out.

"See!" cried Susie. "What makes it do that?"

"Try the cold now," said Uncle Robert. "Here, Donald, hold the bottle in this pail of cold water."

"The rubber is going down," said Donald in a moment. "It is going right into the bottle."

"Does the air in the bottle pull the rubber in with it?" asked Susie.

"But, Uncle Robert," said Donald, "what if wagon tires,

apples, and air do swell up when they are hot? I don't see what all that has to do with the thermometer."

"I think I see," said Frank. "Why wouldn't this gray stuff in the thermometer get bigger when it's hot, if everything else does?"

"What is it that moves up and down in the thermometer?" asked Susie. "It is mercury," answered Uncle Robert, "which is sometimes called quicksilver."

"It looks like silver," said Susie, examining it closely.

"Perhaps you can see this better," said Uncle Robert, taking a small bottle of mercury from his pocket and pouring a little into Donald's hand.

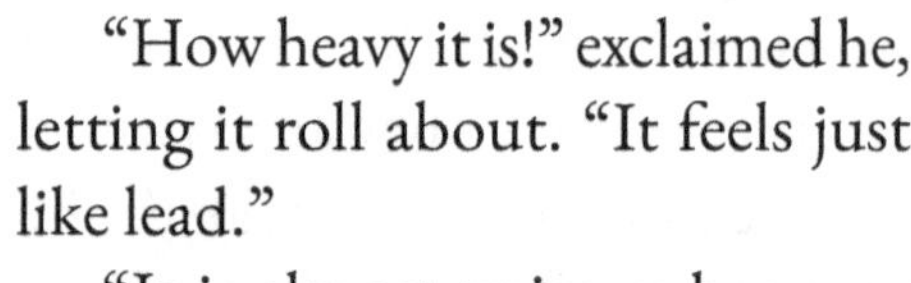

"How heavy it is!" exclaimed he, letting it roll about. "It feels just like lead."

"It is almost twice as heavy as lead," replied Uncle Robert.

"Put it in my hand, Donald," said Susie. "There, you've spilled it on the floor! Just see it run around!"

"Is it always soft like this?" asked Frank.

"No, it becomes hard when it is very, very cold."

"How cold, uncle?" asked Donald, looking at the thermometer.

"Thirty-nine or forty degrees below zero," was the reply. "In the coldest of countries alcohol thermometers are used. It must be much colder than that to freeze alcohol."

"Why is mercury used, uncle?" asked Frank.

"Because it takes a very great heat to make it boil." said Uncle Robert. "Then you have seen how quickly it shows a change of temperature. When it is warm we call it a high temperature, and when it is cold it is called a low temperature."

"That is because the mercury goes up when it is hot, and down when it is cold, isn't it?" said Donald. "I wonder how it would feel if it was forty degrees below zero. See, it is away down to there!"

"Do you remember that day last winter when Peter froze his ears driving to town?" asked Frank. "Well, it was twenty below that day at the post office. I saw it. But father is calling me; I must go."

CHAPTER IV

WITH THE ANIMALS.

"Don't forget to set that hen, Donald," called Mr. Leonard, as he and Frank went away together. "I think there are enough of those Plymouth Rock eggs for one more setting."

"You ought to see our little chickens, Uncle Robert," said Susie. "They are just too cunning for anything."

"When you go to set the hen, Donald," said Uncle Robert, "I will go with you. Then you can show me everything about the barn."

Donald went to the storeroom and soon came back with the eggs.

"There are thirteen," he said, as he joined Uncle Robert in the porch, "but I think she can take care of them. She's one of the largest hens we have."

Then together they went to the henhouse, which stood next to the barn. The chickens, seeing the basket in Donald's hand, ran toward him.

"You needn't think I am going to feed you again so soon," he said. "You have had one breakfast this morning."

Donald always talked to all the animals as though they could understand him.

The mother hens paid no attention. With quiet dignity they walked about, their broods of fluffy little chicks looking like balls

THE POULTRY YARD.

of gold in the sunshine. With a "Cluck! cluck!" each anxious mother called her children to her as her sharp eyes discovered some new dainty. Then the greedy little yellow things ran as fast as their short legs could carry them to be the first to take the good things from the self-sacrificing mother.

"How many little chickens are there?" asked Uncle Robert as they stopped to watch them.

"There are forty-six hatched," said Donald. "Three hens are setting, and this one will make four."

"I see you have some fine turkeys, too," said Uncle Robert.

The big turkey cock spread his tail and strutted about before them as if he understood how much he was admired.

"Mother thinks a great deal of her turkeys," said Donald. "They are much harder to raise than the chickens. But mother knows just how to do it. We don't lose many."

"Have you ducks and geese, too?" asked Uncle Robert.

"Yes," said Donald, "but I don't see any of them about. They must have gone to the creek. There they are," and Donald pointed toward the pasture where a line of white could be seen moving slowly along under the trees.

"They march pretty well, don't they?" said Uncle Robert. "Do they always go that way?"

"Not always," said Donald, "but very often. When that old drake wants to take a swim, he starts and the rest follow. You'd never catch him walking behind."

"As the head of the family I suppose he thinks it is his place to lead," said Uncle Robert, smiling.

Donald laughed. "Wouldn't it be funny," he said, "if father made us follow him that way?"

They found the hen to whom they were carrying the eggs on an empty nest. Donald drove her off that he might put in the eggs, but she was very cross with him for disturbing her. She walked about with her feathers ruffled up, clucking angrily, but eagerly went back to her nest as soon as they were gone. She moved the eggs about with her feet, placed them to suit herself, and contentedly settled down.

Donald then led Uncle Robert into the barn, where old white Nell stood in her stall. Besides Nell there were three strong Normandies in other stalls, and two stalls that were empty.

Mr. Leonard had a very large barn. There was the main floor, running through from the two big rolling doors at either end. The great hay mows on both sides, reached by short ladders, held some of last year's cutting. Under the mows were the stalls for the horses and the stanchions for the cattle. A machine for cutting hay stood on the barn floor.

Under the barn was a deep, roomy cellar, in one corner of which was the sheep pen, lighted by large windows.

Near the barn was a tool house, in which all the tools and machinery were housed during the winter.

"It pays to have a nice warm barn and a good place to keep the tools from rusting," said Uncle Robert. "Do you always keep the horses in the barn when they are not in use?"

"Oh, no," said Donald. "Sometimes they run in the pasture along the creek. The cows and sheep are there now. After the timothy and clover are cut we'll put them in those fields."

"Do you keep many cows?"

"We have six cows and two calves," replied Donald. "Father gave one calf to Frank and one to me. They're beauties. All our cows are Jerseys. Frank and I are going to keep ours until they're grown. Then if they give as much milk as the other cows do—and I'm sure they will—we are going to take it to the creamery and sell it. There's a creamery not far from here."

"Does your father sell the milk there now?" asked Uncle Robert.

"Not now," said Donald. "Mother likes to make the butter herself."

"That's why it is so good," said Uncle Robert.

"Has Susie a calf too?"

Susie, tired of waiting for them to return, had come to see what they were doing. So she answered for herself.

"No, uncle," she said, "but I have the prettiest little lambs you ever saw. They always run to me when they see me coming. Please come out to the lot and see them."

"How many have you?" asked Uncle Robert.

"Two," replied Susie. "They're twins, and are just alike. Their mother is dead. It was cold when they were born. There was snow on the ground. Father brought them into the kitchen in a basket to keep them warm. Mother and I taught them to drink milk, so father gave them to me. I'm going to keep them always."

The Barn.

"Father likes us to have our own things to take care of," said Donald. "I think it's ever so much more fun, don't you, uncle?"

"Yes, indeed," said Uncle Robert. "But you help take care of all the animals, don't you?"

"Oh, yes," replied Donald, "and I like them all; but my calf seems just a little nicer than the rest. I know it isn't any better, really, but I like to think it is my very own."

They stopped to watch the pigeons circling about the pigeon house.

"I love to watch the pigeons," said Susie. "See all the pretty colors in their feathers!"

"Are they very wild?" asked Uncle Robert.

"Oh, no," said Susie, "they're very tame. When we throw grain to them they come down all around us."

"Come and see my pigs!" shouted Donald, who had run ahead and was looking into the pen.

Four white, fat Berkshire pigs lay in the straw, lazily rolling their little eyes toward their friend and feeder. A succession of grunts served for conversation.

"I put in fresh straw every day," said Donald, "so my pigs can keep themselves clean. And they have a patent trough to eat out of."

"I thought farmers in the West let their pigs run in the woods," said Uncle Robert.

"We had a lot of razorbacks for a while, but they didn't pay," said Donald. "Our Berkshires make nice pork."

"How warm the sun is getting!" said Uncle Robert as they turned away from the pigpen.

"The wind is from the southwest," said Donald, looking at the weather vane on top of the barn. "It always gets warmer when the wind is from that direction."

"Uncle," said Susie, "before we begin to plant the seeds let's go and see my lambs."

"You go ahead, and I'll get some salt for the sheep," said Donald. "They always run to me when they see me coming with a pan. They know what that means."

Donald soon joined them with the pan of salt.

"Mother says she can't work in the garden until afternoon," he said, "so we needn't hurry back."

As they entered the pasture the sheep were quietly grazing on the slope of the hill, where the grass was nibbled very short. A few lambs were frisking together at the foot of the hill.

"See the lambs playing, uncle," said Susie. "The two little ones with long tails and black noses are mine. Aren't they cunning? They'll see me in a minute. Then how they will run!"

The quick ears of the sheep caught the sound of their voices.

They raised their heads. Donald held out the pan of salt, shaking it gently. In a moment one of the flock started slowly toward them. Donald stopped under one of the large oak trees that grew on the top of the hill. Uncle Robert and Susie stood beside him. The old sheep came nearer. One by one the rest of the flock began to follow. The lambs stopped playing. Susie held out her hand and called softly, "Come, Sally! Come, Billy!"

The two little lambs switched their tails and started up the hill. Donald sprinkled a little of the salt on the ground. Then the whole flock broke into a run, and the sheep were soon eagerly licking up the salt as Donald scattered it about for them.

Susie's lambs came straight to her side and began to lick her hands and sniff about her dress.

"They think I have something for them," she said. "Let me have some salt, please, Donald."

FEEDING THE SHEEP.

DONALD'S CALF.

Filling each of her hands with salt, she held them out, and the lambs eagerly licked it from the little round palms.

"The cows are down by the creek, uncle," said Donald. "Shall we go to see them? You must see my calf."

"Come on," cried Susie, and began to run as fast as she could go.

The little lambs, always ready for a play, skipped about her. How merrily Susie did laugh as they ran ahead and then turned around with their noses to the ground and their tails in the air, waiting for her to come and catch them!

"They always want me to play with them," she said, quite out of breath, when Uncle Robert and Donald caught up.

"What beautiful cows!" exclaimed Uncle Robert as the little Jerseys lifted their shy faces from the grass to look at them. "I never saw finer ones."

"That is my calf," said Donald, pointing it out with much pride, "and that one over there is Frank's. The only way we can tell them apart is that Frank's has more black on its face than mine has."

"Toot-toot-t-o-o-t!" The sound came from the house.

"There's the horn!" exclaimed Susie. "It must be dinner time."

"So soon?" said Uncle Robert. "How quickly the morning has gone!"

"I tell you I'm hungry," said Donald. "I didn't think of it before, but I'm almost starving."

CHAPTER V

IN THE FLOWER GARDEN.

In the afternoon they all went into the garden. Donald and Mrs. Leonard began at once to set out the tomato plants that had been started in a box. Susie and Uncle Robert walked about, planning where the flower seeds should be planted.

"The verbenas are in this bed," said Susie. "I had them last year. I wish they would begin to come up. Don't you think, uncle, it will be nice to have the mignonette in with them?"

"Yes," replied Uncle Robert, "but where are your nasturtiums?"

"I haven't any nasturtiums," said Susie. "I wish I had. Jennie Wilson's mother had them last year. They bloomed all summer."

"We can send for some seeds and get them in time to plant," said Uncle Robert.

"Oh, thank you, uncle," exclaimed Susie. "How nice! I'll save this big bed for nasturtiums, and the bachelor's buttons can go over there."

"The nasturtiums would do better by the fence and the porch," said Uncle Robert. "They like to climb."

"All right," said Susie; "then we can have this bed for something else."

"Have you any poppies?" asked Uncle Robert, smiling. "Poppies are my favorite flowers."

"Are they, uncle? Then we'll have poppies in this bed."

"Thank you, dear," replied Uncle Robert, taking out his notebook. "We'll send for the poppy seeds, too."

"I think that finishes the beds," said Susie. "Let me see," and, walking down the path, she pointed out where each kind of flower was to grow.

"You might draw it now," said Uncle Robert; "then we'll make no mistake."

"Oh, goody!" cried Susie. "That's what I'll do. Wait until I get a pencil and paper."

"Here is a pencil," said Uncle Robert, taking one from his pocket, "and perhaps this old envelope will do to draw it on."

But Susie thought not. "It's too small," she said. "I'll get a nice piece of paper in a minute."

Away she ran to the house, and soon came back with a large sheet of fresh white letter paper in one hand and Frank's geography in the other.

"I'm going to draw my garden," she called to Donald and her mother, holding up the paper for them to see.

"I'll make the paths first," she said, laying the paper on the geography, and taking the pencil from Uncle Robert. "Then I can put in the beds afterward."

POPPIES

When the paths were drawn, Susie named the beds and marked them off on the paper.

"Please write the names for me, Uncle Robert," she said. "I can't spell all the big words."

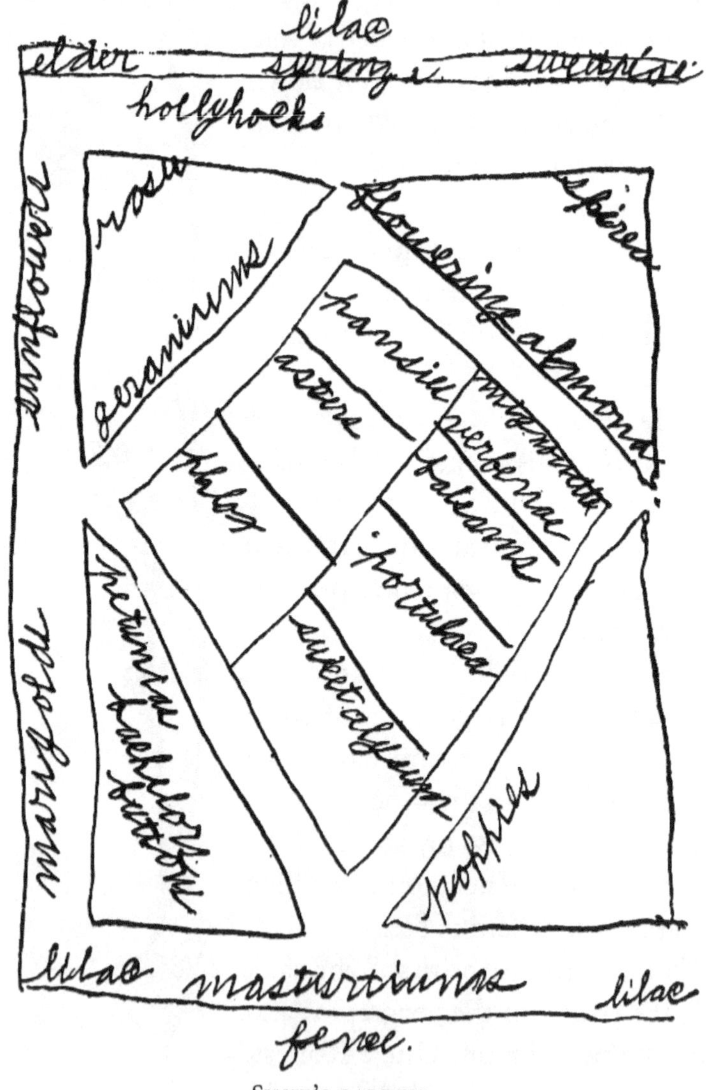

Susie's Garden.

"I will write them on this paper," said Uncle Robert, "and when you see how they look you can write them on your plan."

"Oh, yes," said Susie, "that will be the nicest way."

"See, mother," cried Susie, running to her, "this is my garden. Now I know just what is to be in every bed."

"Where are you going to get poppies?" asked Donald, looking at the plan on the paper.

"Uncle Robert is going to send for the seed," answered Susie. "He likes poppies best of all the flowers. We are going to have nasturtiums, too. They are to grow by the porch and the fence."

"That will be fine, dear," said Mrs. Leonard. "What a beautiful garden we shall have!"

"I can hardly wait," cried Susie, dancing along the walk. "Come, uncle, let's plant what seeds we have now."

"Do we need to do anything to the ground," asked Uncle Robert, "before the seeds are put in?"

"Only rake over the top a little," said Susie, taking up her rake and going to work. "It has been spaded. See how light and fine it is underneath! Ugh! I wish the old worms would keep out!"

"Don't be too hard on the worms," said Uncle Robert. "They are your best helpers."

"I don't see how that is, uncle," said Susie, looking up in surprise.

"You just said the soil was light and fine," said Uncle Robert. "Don't you know you have to thank the worms for keeping it so?"

"Are you sure, uncle?" asked Susie. "I thought the worms ate the plants."

"The earthworms never eat the plants," said Uncle Robert. "They eat the soil, and so keep it worked over. It is the cutworm that eats the plants."

Just then Donald came over from the vegetable garden.

"Why, you've only just begun," he said. "We're all through. Don't those tomato plants look nice?"

"Well," said Susie, "you didn't draw your garden. That took a long time, didn't it, uncle? You rake those beds for me, Don, while I put the seeds in."

"I'd just as soon," said Donald, taking the rake. "What goes here?"

"Mignonette," said Susie. "When any one wants to know about my garden now, they can look at the drawing."

Uncle Robert smiled.

"What makes you think you'll have mignonette there?" he asked, as Susie marked a little furrow with a stick in the soft, warm soil.

"Why, these are mignonette seeds," she replied. "I gathered them myself. Don't you think they'll grow, uncle?"

"Certainly I do," replied Uncle Robert.

"It would be a pretty dead seed," said Donald, "that wouldn't grow in this soil."

"Are seeds alive?" asked Uncle Robert, smiling.

"Why, I—I don't know," said Donald, looking puzzled. "I never thought about it. I just said that. They don't look like it, that's a fact, but they surely wouldn't grow if they were dead, would they?"

"Do all seeds grow in the same way?" asked Uncle Robert.

"I never thought about it," said Donald.

"Neither did I," said Susie. "I just know if I plant mignonette, mignonette will grow; and if I plant sweet peas, sweet peas will grow. That's all I ever thought about it."

"Would you like to know?" asked Uncle Robert.

"Oh, yes," said Susie.

"How can we?" asked Donald. "The seeds are in the ground, and we can't see them."

"If Susie is willing to dig up one of her sweet peas," said Uncle Robert, "perhaps it will tell us what it has been doing since she planted it last week."

"Oh, yes," said Susie. "See if you can find one, Don. I put lots in."

Down on their knees went Susie and Donald, and began digging in the soil.

"Here is one," said Donald, "just ready to come up, and another close to it. The tip of it must have been through. See, it is green."

"Wouldn't it be green in the ground?" asked Susie, looking closely at the tiny plant.

"Why, no," said Donald. "Things are never green when they're covered up. It's light that makes things green. Don't you know how yellow the grass gets if a board lies on it, and what yellow stalks the potatoes have when they sprout in the cellar? It must be the light that makes them green."

"Oh, yes," said Susie. "But see how big that pea is! It's about twice as big as it was when I planted it."

"See," said Donald, "the roots grow from the same place that the stem does. I should

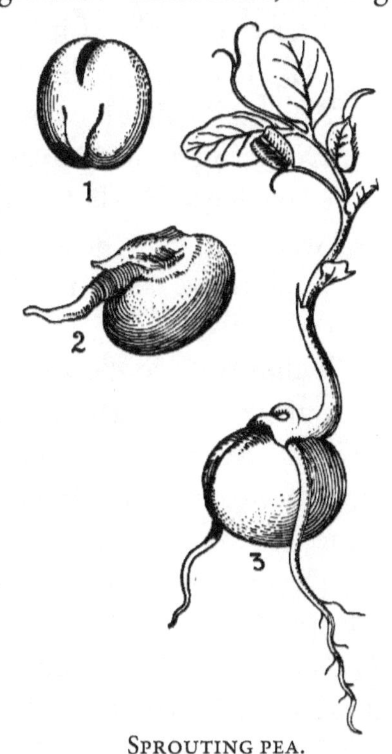

SPROUTING PEA.

think it would be better if one came from one side of the pea, and one from the other."

"What becomes of the rest of the seed?" asked Uncle Robert.

"I don't know," said Susie. "Is it of any use?"

"It is of the greatest use," replied Uncle Robert. "The little pea plant couldn't live without it. It is its food that the mother sweet pea gathered last summer from the soil and air, and stored away in the little round ball for her baby to feed on until it should be big enough to get its own food."

"Do you really mean, uncle," cried Susie, with shining eyes, "that the sweet peas I have planted in that bed are the children of those I had last year?"

"Why not?" asked Uncle Robert, with a smile.

"I never thought of it before," said Susie, looking at the tiny plant in her hand; "but I like it. It seems just like a family."

"And that's what it is," said Uncle Robert.

"Don't you think this baby had better go back to bed?" said Susie, making a deep hole in the ground.

"Wait a moment, Susie," said Uncle Robert.

"Suppose we take it for a visit to the beans, and see if they grow like it."

So they went to the vegetable garden, where they found a great many plants, each with two strong, thick leaves sticking through the soil. Some were quite green and showed a tiny shoot between them. Others were yellow, with only the tips turned green.

"Dig one up, Don," said Susie, "and let's see if it is like the baby pea."

Donald pulled one up, but no bean was to be seen. The stem grew straight into the ground, ending with a little bunch of roots.

"Where's the bean?" asked Susie.

"These two leaves must be the bean," said Donald. "Don't they look like it?" He took a bean from his pocket and held it close to the little plant.

"Well, I never!" cried Susie. "If those two leaves aren't just the bean split open! Are they any good that way, uncle?"

"Yes, indeed," said Uncle Robert, smiling.

"They feed the little bean just as the pea does. But they do even more. What do you think they will do when the sun goes down and the air gets cool?"

"Oh, I know." said Donald. "I've seen them lots of times. They just shut together tight."

"And that keeps the little bud you see in there as warm as you are in your bed."

"Isn't that wonderful?" said Susie. "Why, uncle, it's just as if they could think!"

"The leaves drop off after a while," said Donald. "I often see them lying on the ground."

"Yes," said Uncle Robert. "When the plant is strong enough to take care of itself, their work is done."

"Are there any other plants that make leaves out of the seeds, uncle?" asked Donald.

SPROUTING BEAN.

"Oh, yes," replied Uncle Robert. "Squashes and pumpkins do, and many others. Some have more perfect leaves than these. Let us look at the morning glories by the porch."

"They come up every year by themselves," said Susie.

She ran to her garden, saying, "I'm going to put this pea-baby to bed again. Do you think it will grow, uncle?"

"It may, but it is not good for it to be out of bed too long."

"I'll put a stick by it," said Susie, "so I can watch it. Good-by, baby," giving the ground a little pat; "go to sleep."

MORNING GLORY.

Then she ran after Uncle Robert and Donald.

"How thick the morning glories are!" said Donald. "Some of them have several leaves on, but here is one with only two."

"They don't look as the bean leaves do," said Susie. "The beans are so thick! These have real leaves."

"Yes," said Uncle Robert, "and if you could see them in the seed, you would see these leaves all curled up in their hard coat."

"This one is just putting its head through the ground," said Susie, "and it has part of the shell on it yet."

"It looks as the little chickens do sometimes," laughed Donald, "when they come out of the nest with a piece of the shell sticking to their backs."

"That hard shell is a great protection to the tender plant as it works its way up through the soil," said Uncle Robert.

"If these seed leaves are real leaves,

uncle," asked Donald, "what feeds the baby morning glories?"

"There is plenty of food in the seed around the leaves," said Uncle Robert. "When the seed gets moist in the ground, it becomes so soft that the plant can use it. Have you ever noticed when you were eating corn the little hard bud that grows in each grain close to the cob?"

"Yes, uncle," answered Susie. "That is the sweetest part of the corn."

"That is the part," said Uncle Robert, "from which the new plant grows, and all the rest of the grain is the food stored up for it."

"I wish we had some corn," said Susie, "so we could see it."

"I'll go and get some," said Donald.

"Oh, do, Don," said Susie, "and while he's gone, Uncle Robert, I can plant the rest of my seeds. I have only a few left."

So Donald ran to

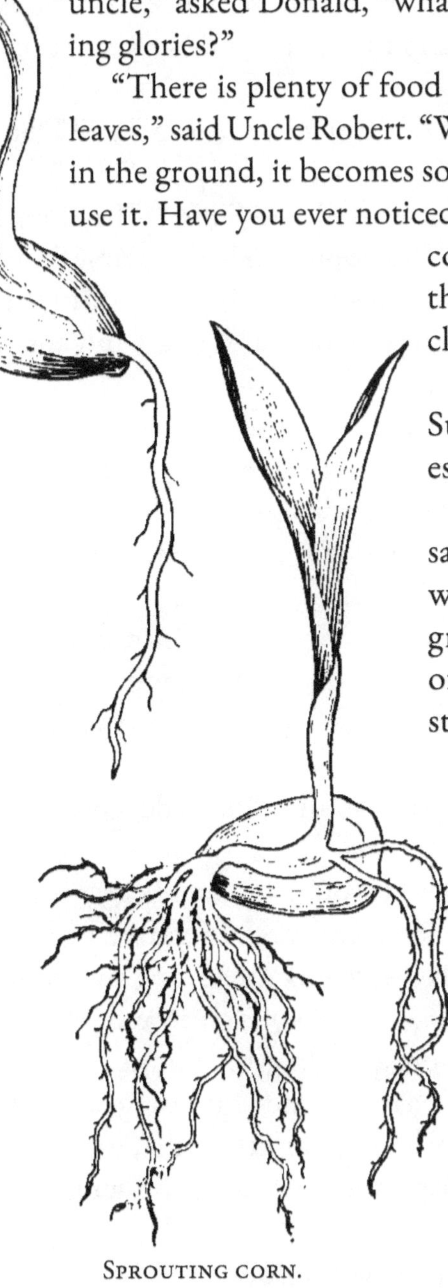

SPROUTING CORN.

the cornfield and Susie went to the garden. When he came back she had finished, and they joined Uncle Robert on the piazza.

"The corn grows out of the side of the seed," said Donald. "See what a big root it has for such a little plant!"

"How pretty those leaves are!" said Susie. "They look like two little green feathers." "Some one else had the same thought, Susie," said Uncle Robert. "Did you ever hear the story the poet Longfellow tells about how the corn came to the Indians? You know it is called 'Indian corn.'"

"No, uncle," said Susie. "Do tell us."

So as they sat beside him on the piazza. Uncle Robert told the story of Hiawatha and Mondamin.

"Hiawatha was a brave young Indian chief," began Uncle Robert, "who wanted to help his people. He knew that there were times when they had no food. In the winter the birds flew away. The 'big sea water,' as they called the great lake, was frozen over, and they could catch no fish. There were no wild berries in the woods.

"'Master of Life,' he cried, 'must our lives depend on these things?'

"He was very unhappy. He could not eat. He lay in his wigwam, fasting and praying for some good to come to his people.

"One evening as he lay watching the setting sun he saw a youth coming toward him. His dress was green and yellow, and over his yellow hair he wore a bright green plume.

"'The Master of Life has sent me,' said the youth. 'I am Mondamin. It is only by hard labor Hiawatha, that you can gain the answer to your prayer. Rise now, and wrestle with me.'

"Hiawatha was weak from fasting, but he did as Mondamin

commanded. Until the sun had set they wrestled together. Then Mondamin went away as silently as he had come.

"A second time he came, and a third. Then he said: "'You have fought bravely, Hiawatha. I shall come once more. You will conquer me. Then you must take off my dress of green and yellow and my nodding plumes. Make a bed in the soft warm earth for me to lie in. Let nothing come to disturb me as I slumber. Only let the sunshine and the rain fall upon me. You must watch beside me, Hiawatha, until my sleep is over.'

"Then he was gone.

"When they wrestled the next night it was as Mondamin had said. He was conquered. Then, day after day, Hiawatha came and watched,

> "'Till at length a small green feather
> From the earth shot slowly upward.'"

"There it is," whispered Susie.

"Sh!" said Donald.

"Then another and another," continued Uncle Robert, "and before long the corn was waving its long, green foliage in the sunshine.

"'It is Mondamin!' cried Hiawatha, 'the friend of man, Mondamin!'"

"What a lovely story!" cried Susie as Uncle Robert finished. "I wish Frank could have heard it."

"We'll find it in your mother's book of Longfellow's poems and let Frank read it," said Uncle Robert.

"Let's tell him about the seeds first," said Donald. "He'll like it better then."

A STALK OF CORN.

CHAPTER VI

SUNLIGHT AND SHADOW.

It was a busy time on the farm. Only when the day's work was over and they were gathered in the sitting-room was there time for the long talks with Uncle Robert that they all enjoyed so much.

"It's wonderful," said Mr. Leonard one evening, looking up from his paper, "how fast the corn is growing. Even the late planting is coming on."

"That's because the weather is so warm," said Donald.

"I wonder what makes it warm?" said Uncle Robert.

"Why, Uncle Robert," exclaimed Susie, "it's spring! That's what makes it warm."

"But what makes it spring, little girl?" asked Uncle Robert.

"Why, it is always spring in May," said Susie.

"I know of a country where it is spring in September," replied Uncle Robert.

"How can it be?" asked Susie. "I thought springtime always came in May."

"What makes us know that it is spring?" asked Uncle Robert.

"Oh, it gets warmer all the time. The birds come, things begin to grow, and the flowers bloom."

"But what makes all this happen just now?"

"It's the sun," answered Donald from the floor, where he

was playing with his great St. Bernard dog, Barri. "You know it rises earlier and sets later every day now than it did a while ago. It's hotter too."

"It goes higher at noon," said Frank. "In the middle of summer it is almost straight over our heads, and in the winter it seems ever so much farther to the south. I've often noticed that."

"So have I," said Donald. "And in the winter the shadows are longer than they are in summer. It must be because the sun isn't so high up."

"Aren't shadows funny?" said Susie. "One day when I was coming in to dinner, just for fun I tried to walk on my shadow, and I could step on my head."

"I've done that lots of times," said Donald. "But it's a strange thing. Sometimes I can step clear over my head—I mean in the shadow—and then again I have to step on it."

"And when you jump," said Susie, "it spoils it. The shadow always jumps too."

"What kind of weather was it when you had to jump to it?" asked Uncle Robert.

"I don't remember," said Donald. "Would the weather make any difference?"

"I remember," said Susie, "because one time when I was jumping that way I fell down and was almost buried in the snow.

"Then it was winter, wasn't it?" asked Uncle Robert.

"It must have been," said Frank.

"And since you told us that the shadows at noon tell why it is warmer in summer than in winter I've been watching them. They get shorter all the time." "How would you like to measure the shadows every day," said Uncle Robert, "and see if you can find out when they are shortest and when they are longest?"

"How can we?" asked Susie. "Shadows are so queer."

"Yes," said Uncle Robert, "shadows are queer, but, if we take one that doesn't jump as yours does, don't you think we can measure it?"

"Of course we can," said Frank. "We can use the house. That always stands still."

"The house might do," said Uncle Robert; "but wouldn't it be better to have a shadow stick?"

"Where can we get one?" asked Donald.

"What is it made of?" asked Frank.

"It is like this," said Uncle Robert, taking paper and pencil from his pocket. "There is one long piece of board, and one short one nailed to the end—so," drawing it on the paper.

"Oh, that's easy enough made," said Donald. "We can do it ourselves right here in the tool house."

"Let's make it to-morrow, Don," said Frank.

"It must be set up some place with the upright end turned toward the south, so that just at noon the shadow of the short piece may fall straight on the board. By drawing a line across the board at the top of the shadow and marking the date on it, we can tell how the length of the shadow changes."

Eskimo scene.

"Uncle," asked Donald, "when it is winter here, is it summer in some other part of the world?"

"Yes," was the reply, "and now that our summer is coming, the people there are beginning to have winter."

"Then," said Frank, "when it gets cooler here in the fall it is growing warmer there, and that would make their spring come in September, wouldn't it? Do you see, Susie?"

"Yes," answered Susie, "but it seems all mixed up. I thought it was the same as it is here all over the world."

"Oh, I didn't," said Donald. "I've read about countries where it is summer all the time, and is so hot that the people don't do anything but lie under the trees and sleep. And there are other countries where it is winter all the time, and the people dress in furs and make their houses of snow and ice. I read all about it in a book once, but it didn't tell why it was so. I knew, of course, the sun had something to do with it."

"Why, you know, Don," said Frank, "we learned all that in our geography at school."

"Yes," said Donald, "but I never thought about that in the geography as meaning any real country."

"What did you think it meant?" asked Uncle Robert.

"Oh," said Donald, "just a lesson in the book."

"Well," said Frank, "I always thought it was some country, but I never knew where. I didn't think much about it after I said the lesson."

"I should think not," said Uncle Robert, not sorry that the teacher had gone away and the school had been closed.

"I wish when books tell things they'd tell why they're so," said Frank.

"Perhaps if we think about these things," said Uncle Robert, "we may be able to answer some of the 'whys' for ourselves."

"We can tell by the thermometer just how warm it is every day," said Susie, "but it won't tell us why."

"The shadow stick may help us there," said Uncle Robert.

"I am afraid I shall forget," said Donald.

"I have some little notebooks in my trunk," said Uncle Robert. "Suppose I give you each one and let you write down what the thermometer and the shadow stick say every day."

"What fun that'll be!" cried Susie. "When may we begin?"

"To-morrow morning, if you like," replied her uncle. "I will get the books for you now."

He went away to his room, and soon returned with the notebooks.

"I'll tell you, uncle," said Frank as he thanked Uncle Robert for his book, "how would it do for each of us to look at the thermometer at a different time of the day?"

"The very thing!" replied Uncle Robert, well pleased. "You are always up early, Frank, so suppose you look at six in the morning, Susie at twelve o'clock, and Donald at six in the evening. How will that do? Then we shall have the record for the whole day."

"I think it will be such fun!" said Susie. "I wonder if our books will be very different."

"What makes you think they will be different?" asked Uncle Robert.

"It's always hotter at noon than it is at night or in the morning," said Susie.

"Do you know," said Uncle Robert, "there are places all over the United States where such records are kept? They are published, and I am to have them sent to me every week."

"I wonder if ours will be like them," said Donald, turning over the pages of his notebook.

"Even if they should be different." said Uncle Robert, "they may be just as true."

"We'll get up early and start the shadow stick the first thing in the morning," said Frank, "so as to have it ready by noon."

"How do you know when it is noon?" asked Uncle Robert.

"We look at the clock," said Susie.

"But noon by the clock is not always noon by the sun," replied Uncle Robert.

"How can that be?" asked Donald.

"It is noon somewhere on the globe every minute of the twenty-four hours," said Uncle Robert. "The sun is always setting and always rising somewhere."

The children were puzzled.

"I don't see how that is," said Donald.

"Let us see if we can find out," said Uncle Robert. "Frank, you stand at the east end of the room, Donald at the west, and Susie in the middle. Now, we'll play that Frank is in New York, Susie here at home in Illinois, and Donald in Denver. I'll take the lamp and be the sun. You are shadow sticks, you know. Now watch the shadows, and see when they point directly north."

Uncle Robert took the lamp and walked slowly from the east side of the room.

"My shadow points north," said Frank as Uncle Robert passed him.

"Now mine does," said Susie.

"And mine last of all," said Donald.

Uncle Robert took out his watch. It was ten minutes past eight.

"That is Susie's time," he said. "Would it be the same in New York, Frank?"

"I think it would be past that," said Frank, "but I don't know how much."

"It is ten minutes past nine by the watch in New York," said Uncle Robert.

"When would it be that time in Denver?" asked Donald.

"In an hour by the watch," said Uncle Robert, "but it would not be the same by the sun."

"Then the watches don't tell the true time, do they?" said Frank.

"The sun's shadows give us the true time," said Uncle Robert. "We will study the shadows, and by and by may learn how the watches and clocks are regulated. But how do you think people told the time before they had clocks?"

"It must have been by the sun," replied Frank.

"I can tell by the sun when it is noon," said Donald, "but I don't see how any one can tell any other hour that way."

"How do you know when it is noon?"

"Why, the sun is highest at noon." said Donald. "and the shadows point straight toward the north."

"Early in the morning they point to the west," said Frank, "and in the evening they point to the east."

"The people who lived in the world many hundred years ago observed the same thing," said Uncle Robert. "There was nothing so strange to them as the rising and setting of the sun. They loved the light that came with it. They feared the darkness that followed its going away. They told many interesting stories to explain this continued appearance and disappearance. Some thought the sun was a king riding through the sky in a golden chariot. Others looked upon it as a god and worshiped it.

"They soon learned that when it went away it was sure to come again, and as they saw how regularly it moved, they felt there must be some power back of it to guide it. Through this they were led to a belief in a Being that controlled all things.

"They watched the shadows, too, and saw them change just as you see them every day. They learned that the shadow is shortest when the day is half gone, and they called that time midday. So, by studying the length and direction of the shadows, they soon became able to judge the time of day.

"Then some one thought to set up a rod and mark the places where the shadow fell at sunrise, at sunset, and at midday. The space in between was divided for the hours. This was called a sun dial and was the first instrument ever made for telling time."

"When was the first one made?" asked Frank.

"That is not known," replied Uncle Robert, "but we read in the Bible of the sun dial of King Ahaz, who lived about eight hundred years before the time of Christ. That is the first record we have of one."

"How was it made?" asked Donald.

"I do not know how the one King Ahaz used was made," said Uncle Robert, "but I can show you how one looked that I saw in an old garden in England. This," drawing a half circle, "is the dial on which the hours were marked. Around this dial there was a border, much cracked, and crumbling away, but I could read the words, 'The sun guides me, the shadow you.' The rod, or gnomon, as it is sometimes called, stood just halfway between the ends. Where would the noon shadow fall, Susie?"

"In the middle, wouldn't it?" answered Susie.

"And the morning shadow would fall on the west and the evening shadow on the east side," said Frank.

"Now we'll put in the shadow stick," said Uncle Robert, drawing a triangle on the paper.

"Why don't you make it stand up straight?" asked Donald.

"The shadow does not tell the truth," said Uncle Robert, "unless it points in the same way that the north pole does, and that, we know, points to the north star. I will explain this some other time."

SUN-DIAL

"Couldn't we make a sun dial?" asked Donald. "I don't believe it would be very hard."

"You could make one easily," answered Uncle Robert.

"But let's have the shadow stick first," said Frank.

Susie went to the window and looked out at the clear star-lighted sky.

"Uncle," she said, "the stars all look alike to me, only some are little and some are big. How can people know them by their names?"

"Just as anything else is known, dear," replied Uncle Robert, "by close and careful study."

"I wish we could study the stars," said Frank.

"We will some time," replied Uncle Robert. "Come out on the piazza now, and I will show you the north star. That will be a good beginning."

CHAPTER VII.

THE BAROMETER.

One day when it was Donald's turn to go for the mail he found among Uncle Robert's letters a small paper. On the wrapper he read "United States Weather Report."

It had come. There was already quite a line of figures in each of their notebooks. Now they could see what this other record was like. As he left the post office he stopped to look at the old thermometer beside the door. Then he mounted Nell and rode down the village street and out into the pleasant country road.

Uncle Robert was waiting for him on the porch, and as Donald rode away to the barn, after giving him the mail, he heard him say:

"Here, Frank, is the Weather Report. Open it and look at it while I read my letters."

Donald took off the saddle and gave the horse her supper. Then he hurried back to see what Frank had found on the inside of the important-looking wrapper. It proved to be a map with queer, crooked lines all over it, but it did not look at all interesting.

"Here it says temperature," said Frank, pointing to a list of figures in the corner. "Perhaps this is what we want."

"I don't see any numbers there like mine," said Donald, taking his notebook from his pocket.

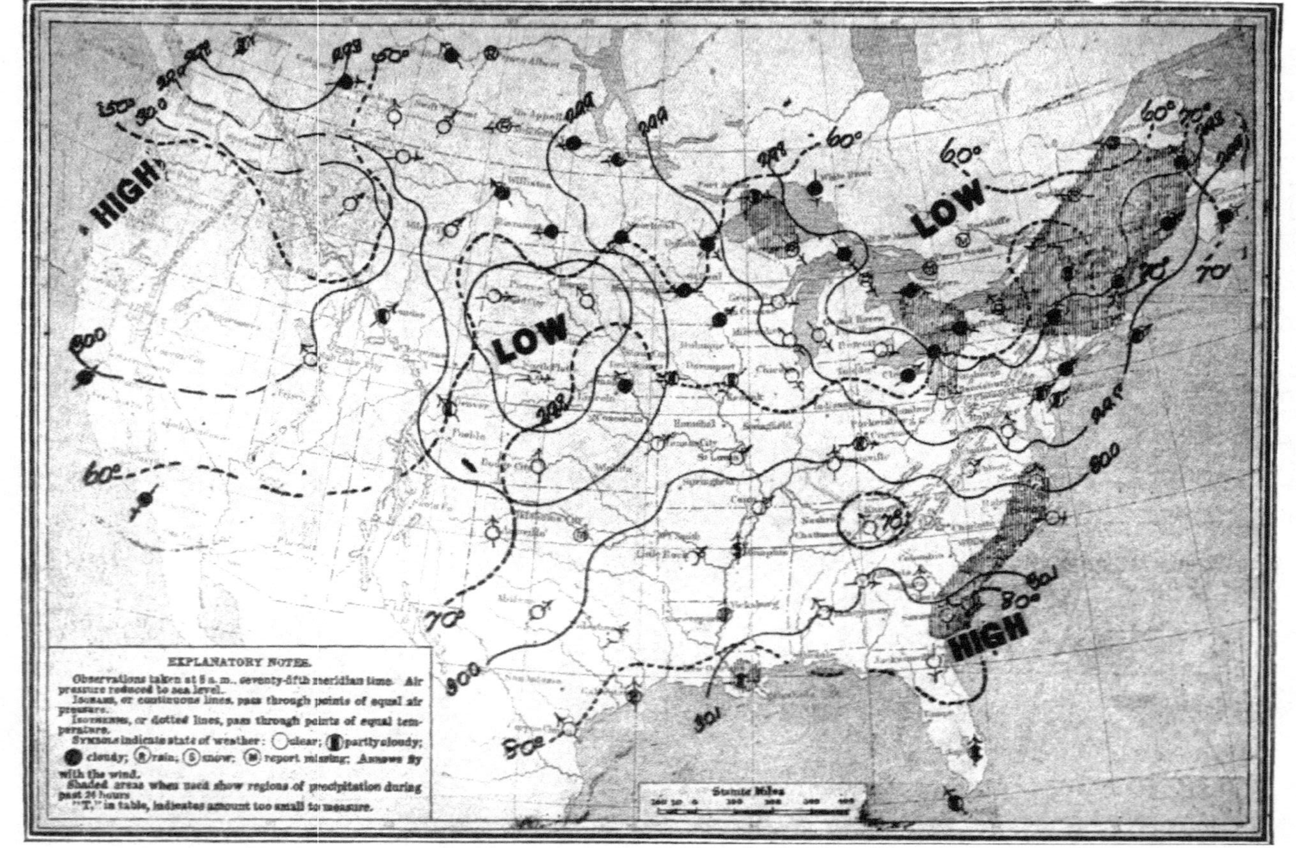

United States weather map.

"Let me help you," said Uncle Robert, laying aside his letters and coming to where they sat on the steps.

They made room for him, and, as he took the map, he explained:

"This, you see, is a map of the United States. These dotted lines tell about the temperature. For instance, look at this one which is marked fifty degrees. At every place in the country that is touched by this line on the map the thermometer stood at fifty degrees at the time the map was made."

"See," said Susie, "how crooked the line is. Why isn't it straight, uncle?"

"Because," was the reply, "as I told you, it goes wherever the temperature was fifty degrees. You remember, the first day we had our thermometer, we found that there are many things which affect the tem-

Thursday 69°

Friday 73°

Saturday 70°

Sunday 61°

Monday 60°

Tuesday 66°

Wednesday 68°

Thursday 69°

Friday 71°

Saturday 72°

SUSIE'S NOTEBOOK

perature. At some places along this line there are prairies, at others forests, at others lakes, and here," pointing to the map, "there are high mountains. All of these things affect the temperature, and that, of course, changes the direction of the line."

"You say Chicago is the nearest station to us, uncle," said Frank, looking down the temperature column. "My record for that day is not so very different from the one given here for Chicago."

"Which shows that yours is probably as nearly correct as this is," said Uncle Robert, with an encouraging smile.

"But I haven't one number in my book like that," said Susie, looking disappointed. "I don't see why."

"I do," replied Uncle Robert. "You make your record at noon, and of course, it is warmer then. That is what your book says, does it not?"

"Yes," said Susie, "every number in my book is more than that one."

"That is right," was the reply, "for this record was made at eight o'clock in the morning, which is nearer Frank's hour than it is yours. So we would expect his to be nearer like this than yours, wouldn't we?"

"It isn't like mine either," said Donald.

"We may have one some time that will be more like yours," said Uncle Robert, "for these records are made at eight in the evening as well as in the morning."

"Uncle," said Frank, looking closely at the map, "here it says 'High,' and there it says 'Low.' What does that mean?"

"It means," said Uncle Robert, "that here there is a low barometer, and there the barometer is high."

"Barometer," said Donald. "What is a barometer, uncle? Is it like a thermometer?"

Experiment No. I.

"Well, not exactly," was the reply. "With the thermometer, you know, we tell the temperature of the air, and with the barometer we tell how heavy it is."

"How heavy the air is!" exclaimed Susie. "How funny! Why, uncle, air doesn't weigh anything, does it?"

"More than you think, little girl," said Uncle Robert, smiling. "But perhaps we can prove whether it does or not. Frank, will you get a pail of water? Donald, see if you can find a cork some place; and Susie, run in and get a tumbler."

When all was ready Uncle Robert asked Frank to fill the pan with water, and Donald to put the cork into it.

"There," said Donald, as the cork floated about on the pan of water.

"But I want the cork on the bottom of the pan," said Uncle Robert, "not on the top of the water."

"It won't stay there," declared Donald, pushing it into the water again and again with his finger. "It is too light. Corks always float."

"How can we make it go to the bottom?"

No one could tell. The children looked puzzled.

"Let us see what this will do," and, taking the glass from Susie's hand, Uncle Robert turned it over the cork, pressed it down into the water as far as it would go, and held it there. Looking through the glass, they could see the cork lying on the bottom of the pan.

"Why, Uncle Robert!" exclaimed Susie, "what—how—"

"It's the glass that does it," declared Donald.

"But the glass doesn't touch the cork," objected his uncle.

"There's air in the glass," said Frank, who had been looking at it quietly as the others talked. "That is what presses it down."

"If it's air," said Donald, "why didn't it go down before the glass was put over it? There was just as much air about it then, and more, too."

"Let go of the glass, uncle," said Frank, "and see what it will do."

Uncle Robert did so, and the glass instantly turned over, while a big bubble of air escaped through the water.

"There," said Frank, smiling, "I told you so!"

"Then air only presses on things when there is something like the glass to hold it down. Is that so, uncle?" asked Donald.

"Let us see," was the reply.

Filling the glass with water, he placed a piece of paper over it, and quickly turned it upside down. Not a drop of water fell from the glass. The paper, now beneath the water, stayed there as though glued.

"Uncle," said Frank, "is it truly the air that holds the paper on and keeps the water in the glass? If it presses that way everywhere, why don't we feel it?"

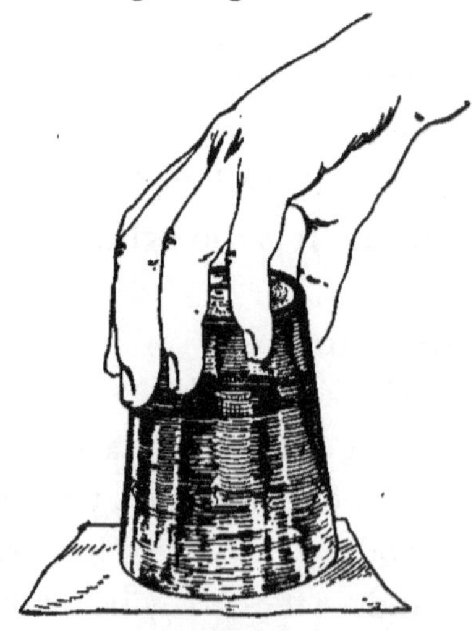

AIR PRESSURE. EXPERIMENT NO. 2.

"It is because it presses

equally in every direction," replied Uncle Robert. "Put your hand in this pail of water. Do you feel it pressing on your hand?"

"No," said Frank.

"Place it lower in the water. Does it feel any heavier now?"

"Not at all," answered Frank.

"But you know that the water is heavy. Lift the pail, Donald."

"It is heavy," said Donald, setting it down. "I don't see why Frank didn't feel a little of the weight of it when his hand was under all the water."

"It is this way," explained Uncle Robert. "The water pressed on his hand from below as much as from above, and the same on both sides. When you lifted it you felt its weight pressing downward only. Now it is just so with the air. It presses with such equal pressure that we do not realize its weight. It is only when it presses harder from one direction than from another that we feel it."

"That's when the wind blows, isn't it, uncle?" asked Donald.

"Yes, my boy," was the reply. "You can see how it is out among the trees now."

"But, uncle," said Donald, "how can the air be weighed if it presses the same in all directions? It was only when I lifted the whole pail of water that I felt how heavy it was. The air can't be weighed if it presses up just as much as it does down."

"But if in some way it could be shut off so that it would only press in one direction?"

"It might be," answered Donald, "but I don't see how."

Uncle Robert told Susie to put the glass in the water so that it would all be below the surface, and, without taking it from the water, to turn it upside down. She did so, and then began to lift it slowly out of the water.

"See," cried Susie, "the water comes with it. The glass is full. Could I lift it clear out that way?"

"Try it," said Uncle Robert, smiling.

But no; when the edge of the glass came out of the water in the pail, down went the water with a splash.

"I see how it is," said Frank, who had watched it closely. "There wasn't any air in the glass to keep the water out, as there was when we turned it over the cork, so the water stayed in it."

"But what made it come up out of the pail?" asked Donald. "There wasn't any air under it to press it up."

"Would the air pressing on the water around the glass make it do so, uncle?" asked Frank, placing the glass in the water and raising it as Susie had done. "It seems as if it might be that."

"That is what it is," replied his uncle. "The air pressing on the water in the pail forces it into the glass, where there is nothing to keep it from rising."

"If the glass was longer would the water stay in it just the same?" asked Donald.

"Yes," was the reply. "If there was no air in the glass it would have to be very many times as long as this glass is to hold the water that would rise if it had a chance. But come, let us sit down on the steps again, and I will tell you about it."

When they were settled he continued:

"Over two hundred and fifty years ago there lived a man named Galileo, who learned a great many wonderful things by studying the stars and doing just such things as we have been doing. It was he who made the first thermometer. But there was one question that he could not answer. He found that in a hollow glass tube, closed at one end, water would rise thirty-four feet high, but no higher. He could not tell why. A pupil

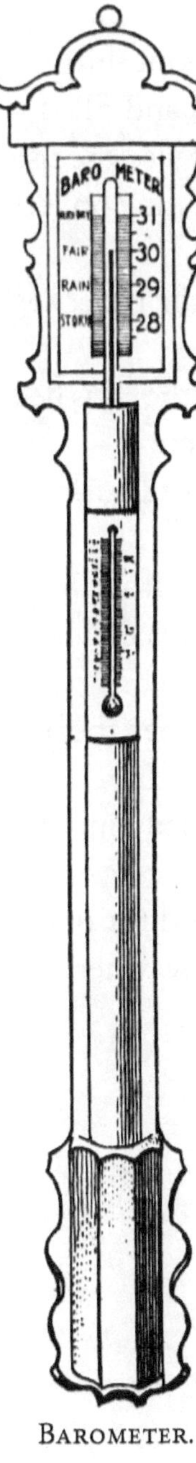

BAROMETER.

of his thought he would try the same thing with the heaviest liquid known——"

"That was mercury, wasn't it, uncle?" interrupted Donald.

"Yes; he used mercury, and found that it rose in the tube just thirty inches. He knew that the mercury was thirteen and six-tenths times as heavy as the water, so he felt sure that it was the pressure of the air that made them both rise in the tube, for thirty-four feet is just thirteen and six-tenths times thirty inches. But they wanted to see if it was really the air, so they took the tube up on a high mountain."

"What difference would that make?" asked Susie.

"Look at the woodpile out there," said her uncle. "Where do you think the weight of the wood would be the greater? On the ground or halfway to the top?"

"On the ground, of course," answered Susie.

"Well, they found it was the same with the air. As they went up the mountain the mercury in the tube fell."

"That showed that the weight on it was less, didn't it, uncle?" said Frank. "I think that was a very wonderful discovery, don't you?"

"It was, indeed," replied Uncle Robert, "and that is how the first barometer was made."

"Is that what a barometer is?" asked Donald.

"Yes," was the reply, "simply a glass tube about thirty-three or thirty-four inches long, closed at the top, and filled with mercury. It is then placed in a small open cup, called the cistern, into which the mercury flows until the air pressing on it there will let it fall no farther."

"Does it always stay at the same height in the tube?" asked Donald.

"Oh, no," his uncle answered. "Some days the air is heavier than others, and so presses harder on the mercury."

"That would make it rise, wouldn't it?" asked Susie.

"Yes, dear."

"So, uncle," said Frank, taking up the Weather Report, "where it says 'High' here, it means that the air is heavier than where it says 'Low.' Is that it?"

"That's right," replied Uncle Robert; "and when the barometer is low we know there will be a storm."

"Well"—and Donald stood up and stretched himself—"I wish I could see a barometer."

"You shall," said Uncle Robert "I will send for one. You may carry the letter to the post office to-morrow when you go for the mail."

CHAPTER VIII

A WALK IN THE WOODS.

It was a beautiful Sunday afternoon. The sun had marked its shortest shadows. They were now pointing toward the northeast.

The family had returned from the little village church. Dinner was over, and they had all gone into the cool, shady piazza. Mrs. Leonard and Susie had settled themselves cozily in one corner and were reading together. Mr. Leonard was nodding over the pages of his weekly newspaper. Frank, stretched out on the settee, was absorbed in a new book, while not far away Donald lay under the spreading branches of a spruce tree with Barri by his side. Uncle Robert stood gazing at the green woods, which looked so cool and inviting.

"'The groves were God's first temples,'" he said to himself, and then, turning to the others, asked, "Who wants to go for a walk?"

"I do," said Frank, springing up. "Come on, Don. Don-ald!" he called, "we're going for a walk."

"You'd better come with us," said Uncle Robert to Mrs. Leonard.

"I'll get your hat, mother," cried Susie eagerly, running into the house.

"Shall we go to the cornfield?" asked Mr. Leonard, picking up his straw hat.

"I think it would be cooler in the woods," said Mrs. Leonard.

"Oh, yes," said Donald, "let's go up the creek to the pond."

The country was in the full glory of early summer. Just beyond the rich green of the great cornfield could be seen the peaceful river. The yellowing grain on the upland waved gently in the breeze. Under the wide-spreading oak trees in the pasture the cows were lazily chewing their cuds. A feeling of quiet pleasure filled the air.

"I planted all these trees," said Mr. Leonard as they walked under the maples that grew on either side of the road. "It is wonderful how they have grown. They were like little sticks when I set them out."

"The one at the end of the row," said Mrs. Leonard, "was planted the day Frank was born."

"It is the largest of them all," said Frank.

"That's because it was planted first," said Susie. "I have a tree, too, uncle."

"So have I," said Donald. "It is the spruce in the front yard."

"We call them our birthday trees," said Susie. "Mine is the elm by the corner of the porch."

"That is a very nice custom," said Uncle Robert. "But the trees grow faster than you do."

"They don't have anything to do but grow," said Donald.

When they reached the bridge they paused to look up and down the creek valley. Through the trees they caught glimpses of the shining river and the waving corn. The creek, a little stream, flowed between the two gentle slopes that formed its valley.

"There's a gate under this bridge, uncle," said Donald, "to keep the cows from going down the creek to the cornfield. In

THE BRIDGE.

the fall, after the corn is cut, we open it, and let them go to the river."

"How pleasant it is in here!" said Uncle Robert as they walked farther into the wood.

"Just see how damp the ground is under these dead leaves!" said Susie as she pushed them back from a little violet that she was trying to pick with a long stem. "Poor little flowers! How do they ever get through all these leaves? It would be so much easier for them if it was just green grass."

"But then there wouldn't be any flowers," said Mr. Leonard, "or at least they would be very different."

"It's the leaves that make the soil so rich," said Frank, digging into the ground with a stick. "See how they are mixed all through it!"

"Do you know the names of all these trees?" asked Uncle Robert.

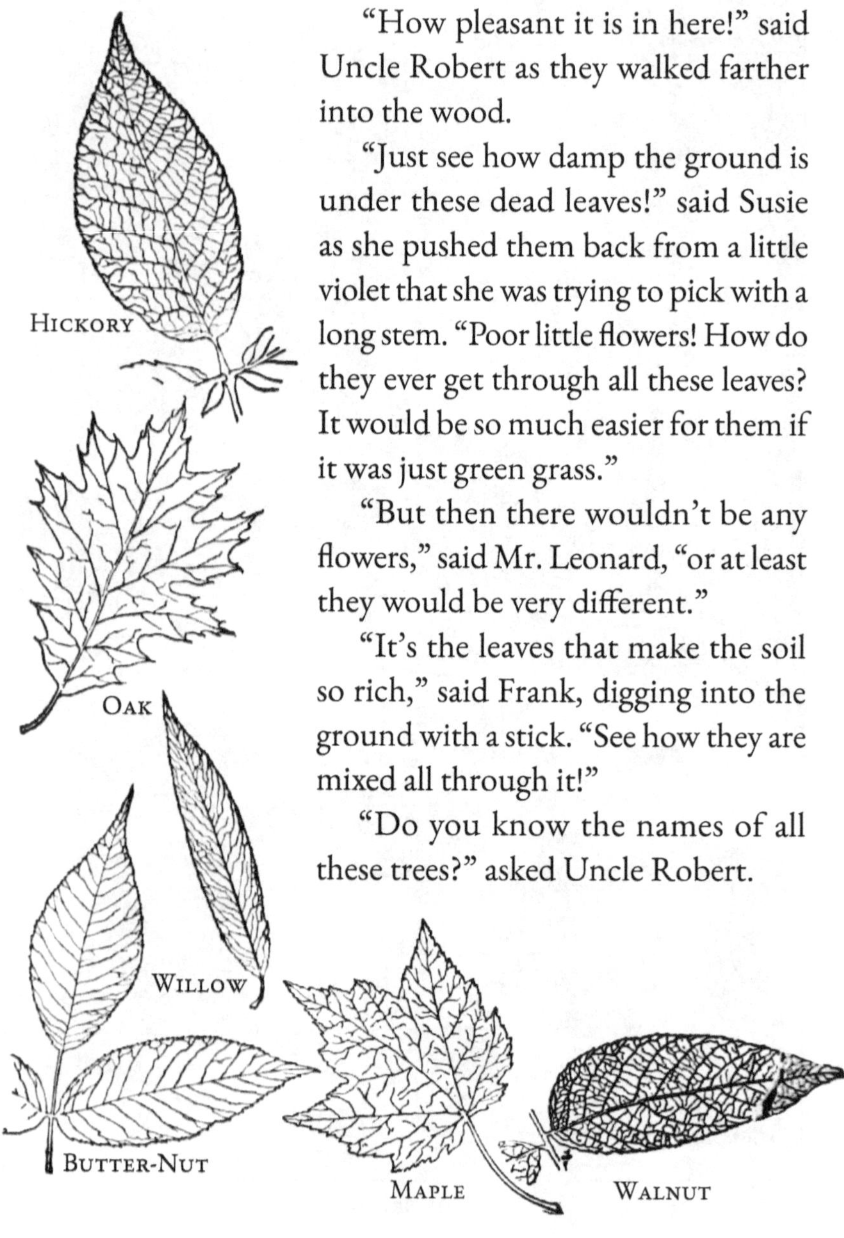

"I do," said Frank. "I can tell every tree in the wood."

"How?" asked Uncle Robert.

"By the leaves is the easiest way," said Frank, "but I know some trees by the bark."

"I can tell them by the leaves," said Donald. "Try me."

So as Uncle Robert pointed to them Donald called them all by name. There were oaks and maples, hickories, walnuts, and butternuts, and close to the creek the overhanging willows.

"Can you tell a tree by its shape when you look at it from a distance?" asked Uncle Robert.

"I can tell the willows and poplars," said Frank, "and maples, too."

"The trees in the pasture have a different shape from those in the woods," said Uncle Robert. "I mean trees of the same kind. How do you explain that?"

"Why, the trees in the pasture have a chance to spread out," said Donald. "There isn't so much room in here."

"But these trees are taller," said Frank, "and they are straighter, too."

"Can you tell the direction of the winds that blow the strongest and longest by the shape of the trees?" asked Uncle Robert.

"I never thought of that," said Frank.

"The wind doesn't blow in the woods," said Donald.

"When we get out into the pasture we'll notice the trees there," said Mr. Leonard.

"Isn't this a tiny tree?" said Susie. "I wonder what it is."

"That's an oak," said Frank. "The leaves tell that."

"Oaks grow from acorns," said Donald. "I'm going to dig this up and see if it grows like the seeds in the garden."

"What a long root it has!" said Susie as Donald dug about

it. "Don't take it out, Don. Put the dirt back and let it grow to be a tree."

"How long will it be before it gets as big as these trees, uncle?" asked Frank.

"A great many years. Perhaps your father can tell about how old some of these trees are."

"I have cut some," said Mr. Leonard, "that were about a hundred years old."

"Why, father," exclaimed Susie, "how could you tell?"

"Do you know how the end of a log looks when it is sawed off straight?"

"I do," said Frank. "There are light and dark rings in it."

"Well," was the reply, "one of these rings grows every year."

"So if you count the rings you can tell how old the tree is," said Donald. "Isn't that great!"

"What time of the year do the trees grow the most?" asked Uncle Robert.

"In the spring I should think," said Frank. "That's when the sap begins to run."

"What is sap?"

"It must be the water that the trees take up from the ground," said Frank.

"We've tapped some maple trees for sap," said Donald.

"And we could see it run right out of the tree," said Susie.

"I've told the children how we used to

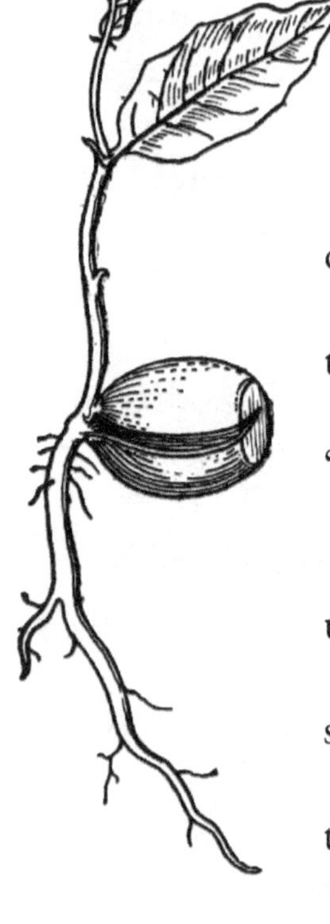

Oak sprout.

make maple sugar in New England,"

END OF A LOG.

said Mrs. Leonard. "Do you remember, Robert, what a quantity of sap it took to make just a little sugar?"

"Yes, and I also remember how long I thought it took to boil it down into the wax I was so fond of."

"About thirty gallons of sap can be taken from one tree each year," said Mr. Leonard.

"But I should think that would hurt the tree," said Frank.

"No," replied Uncle Robert, "for the hole they make is only about an inch across. If they were to cut all around the tree, you see, it would stop the running of the sap and kill the tree."

"That is called girdling," said Mr. Leonard. "They used to clear off hundreds of acres of land in that way when this country was first settled. Instead of cutting down the trees, they girdled them near the ground. In a very short time they died, because they could get no food from the earth. The dead trees lost their strength, and a strong wind would blow them over. Then they were piled up and burned."

"How do you know when a tree is dying?" asked Uncle Robert.

"The leaves turn yellow," said Donald.

"But the leaves turn yellow in the fall," said Frank, "and the trees do not die."

"The leaves of my spruce don't turn yellow in the fall," said Donald. "They stay green all winter."

"What makes the leaves green?" asked Uncle Robert.

No one answered.

"What is the color of the potato sprouts in the cellar?"

"Yellow," said Susie.

"When you take up a board that has lain on the grass, what is the color of the grass?"

"Yellow," said Donald.

"Why?" asked Uncle Robert.

"Because they don't get any light," said Frank.

"You know why we put our plants in the south window in winter?" said Mrs. Leonard.

"Oh, yes," said Susie, "because the sun shines in at that window."

"Warmth and water and air help trees and plants to grow," said Uncle Robert, "but without sunlight their leaves would be yellow and their stems and branches weak. The greatest forests on earth are where it is very hot and moist. The sun is a wonderful artist, and every leaf it paints makes the tree stronger."

"But what makes the leaves turn yellow and red just before they fall off?" asked Frank. "Does the sun paint them then?"

"That is a question that no one has been able to answer," replied his uncle.

"But how can the sap flow up the tree?" said Donald. "I should think it would run down."

"It would unless there was something to draw it up," said Uncle Robert.

"I suppose the sun does that, too," said Frank.

"Where does it go after it reaches the leaves?" asked Uncle Robert.

"Why, back again," said Susie.

"No, it doesn't go back—not a drop," laughed Uncle Robert.

"Does it dry up?" asked Donald.

"What do you mean by drying up?"

"It evap-o-rates," said Donald, who liked to use large words.

"Does it all go into the air?" asked Frank.

"I want you to answer these questions yourselves, children. What do you see on the corn leaves in the early morning?"

"Drops of water; but that is dew, isn't it?" asked Frank.

Uncle Robert had a way of stopping or changing the subject when he had asked certain questions. He knew that the children would think of them again and try to answer them.

"Let's sit down on this log," said Susie. "I want to fix my flowers."

As they sat there squirrels ran up the trunks of the trees and laughed at them from the branches.

"That is a good shot," said Frank, pointing to a large fox squirrel. "But he knows we won't kill him, and that's the reason he shows himself."

"Is it right to shoot the pretty squirrels, Uncle Robert?" asked Susie.

"I thought so when I was a boy. I shot a great many of them then. It was fun for me, and I felt very proud when I brought home half a dozen grays.

"Once I went home from the city for a sum-mer's rest. I took my gun for a stroll in the oak woods where I had shot

THE SQUIRREL

so many squirrels. I put my gun against a tree and lay down upon the leaves. Soon I was fast asleep. I dreamed of a group of merry, laughing children running, scampering, playing."

"Then my dream became real—not children, but the gray coats, five or six of them, close to me, were running up the trees, jumping from limb to limb, scampering over the ground, chasing each other, laughing as squirrels laugh, and screaming as squirrels scream. I watched the happy playmates, brim full of fun. I have never shot a squirrel since."

CHAPTER IX.

THE BIRDS AND THE FLOWERS

The little family party strolled on through the beautiful woods, following the windings of the creek that was now a tiny stream.

Here and there were little holes hollowed out by the spring floods. Miniature falls gurgled over dead leaves. Graceful ferns fringed the creek's banks. Mosses covered the boulders.

Through the foliage danced the rays of the bright sun, cast-

THE CREEK IN THE WOODS

BLACKBIRDS.

ing wavering shadows over the leaf-covered ground.

"Here is the pond!" cried Susie.

But the pond that formed the reservoir of the creek was now nearly drained, and in place of water there was a swamp filled with reeds, rushes, and grasses. A small clear pool remained in the center.

On the tall reeds swaying to and fro piped a family of blackbirds, busily chattering to each other. Overhead in the cloudless sky floated a huge hawk.

"In the spring this ground is all covered with water; it makes quite a large lake," said Mr. Leonard.

"You thought of draining off the water and turning the pond into a cornfield, didn't you, father?" asked Mrs. Leonard.

"Yes," said Mr. Leonard; "by digging a ditch or making the channel deeper at the outlet, this would become dry land the year around. The soil is deep and rich—better even than the bottom land."

"That would spoil the creek, wouldn't it, father?" asked Frank.

"Yes, it would run in the spring only," said Mr. Leonard.

"Where would the cattle drink in the summer?" asked Donald.

"That's the difficulty. The swamp holds enough to keep the cattle in water all summer."

"Would the corn more than pay for the loss of the water?" asked Frank.

"Yes, I think so," answered his father.

"But it would spoil my beautiful creek," said Susie. "Don't do that."

"If this swamp were in New England," said Uncle Robert, "the farmers would dig out this rich mud for their poor land."

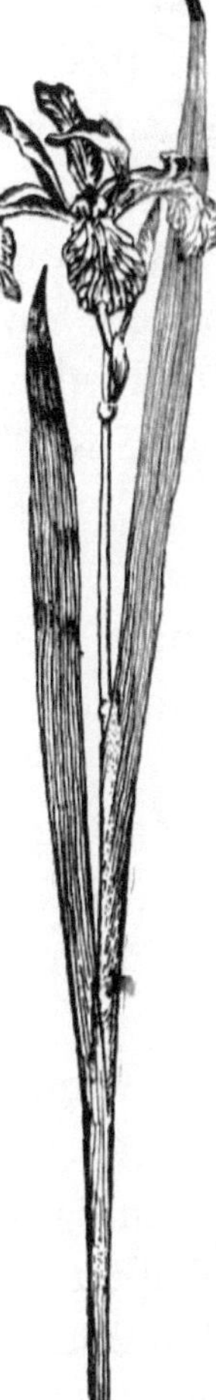

"Oh," cried Susie, "the blue flags are almost in bloom!"

"There is one all blossomed out," said Donald. "I'll get it."

The boys took an old log and threw it across the wet place, and Donald, balancing himself carefully, went out and picked the blooming flag with its buds.

"Thank you, Donald," said Susie, as he handed her the pretty flowers. "I'll put the buds in water and they will open."

"Do you know the names of all the flowers in your bouquet?" asked Uncle Robert.

"Every one of them," said Susie. "This is phlox. There is ever so much of it in the woods now. And this is a trillium. Isn't it big and white? Here is another, only it is red."

"We used to call the red ones 'wake-robin' in New England," said Uncle Robert. "I thought they came earlier than the white ones."

BLUE FLAG.   "They do," said Susie. "They've been here a long time."

WILD GERANIUM.

"The violets are just as pretty as when I came, aren't they?" said Uncle Robert. "Do they stay all summer?"

"Not quite," replied Susie. "But they stay a long time in the woods."

"What is this?" asked Uncle Robert, pointing to a pale-pink flower on a hairy stem, surrounded by rough green leaves.

"That's a wild geranium," said Susie; "but do you think it looks much like a geranium? I don't."

"No, but here is a seed pod," said Uncle Robert. "It looks like the seed of the geranium that grows in the garden. Perhaps that is what gave it the name."

"I have a flower that you haven't, Susie," said Mrs. Leonard, holding it up for them to see.

"Oh," cried Susie, "a yellow lady's slipper! I didn't know they were out yet. Where did you find it?"

"I picked it on the bank near the creek while you were talking about the trees," replied her mother.

"I wish I could find a pink one," said Susie, looking around.

"Isn't it too early for them?" asked Uncle Robert.

"They come about the same time as the yellow ones," said Donald, "but we don't find very many of them."

"I like the Indian name for that flower," said Mr. Leonard.

"Do you mean moccasin flower, father?" asked Frank. "I like that too."

"Why don't we call it that?" asked Donald.

"Lady's slipper is easier to remember," said Susie.

"Here are some bluebells, Susie," said Frank, holding up a handful of the dainty, graceful blossoms. "Give some to mother, and you may have the rest."

"How many blue flowers we have!" said Susie. "There aren't any red ones excepting the red trillium, and that's so dark it isn't really red."

"It's more purple than red," said Donald.

"This isn't the time of the year for red flowers," said Mrs. Leonard. "They come later in the summer and in the fall."

"I wonder why there are no red ones in the spring," said Susie.

"I saw painted cups along the edge of the timothy meadow yesterday," said Donald.

"Oh, did you, Don? Were they truly red, or just yellow?"

"No, they were in bloom. They were red."

YELLOW LADY'S SLIPPER.

Moccasin flower.

"Let's go home that way," said Susie, "and get some."

"I wish all the people in New York could know how restful these woods are," said Uncle Robert, breathing a long breath of the sweet, pure air.

"It always seems to me more quiet in the woods on Sunday than on any other day," said Mrs. Leonard.

"Do the birds know when it is Sunday?" asked Susie.

"If they do," said Uncle Robert, "those blue jays must have forgotten."

"Just hear how they scream!" said Frank.

"They must be up to their usual trick," said Mr. Leonard, "of tormenting some other bird."

"Listen!" said Donald. "It's a sparrow hawk they're after. That's the sparrow hawk's cry, but it's a blue jay that made it. They always mimic them when they chase them. I've watched them lots of times."

"I wish we could see them now!" said Frank. "The hawk will turn on them soon. Then they'll change their tune."

"They are having a good time shouting and screaming to each other," said Susie. "What a horrid noise they make!"

"They scare away the other birds," said Donald.

"How many birds do you know?" asked Uncle Robert.

"I know all the birds that come around the house and

BLUE JAY.

the barn," said Donald. "There are the robins, sparrows, pewees, wrens, swallows, and martins. Then there are the birds in the fields—the larks and the crows. The names of some of the little birds in the woods I do not know."

"You have left out the woodpeckers," said Frank, "and the thrushes and catbirds."

"And the cherry birds, that look like canaries," said Susie.

"Get up early in the morning, just as the sun is rising, and you will hear a chorus," said Mrs. Leonard. "It is a regular morning praise meeting."

"The oriole, or golden robin, is the handsomest bird of all," said Donald.

"A great many birds come in the spring which stay only a few days," said Frank.

"Where do they come from, and where do they go?" asked Uncle Robert.

"They come from the south, I suppose, where it is warmer. I wonder how they know when it is time to start," said Frank.

"And which way to go," added Donald.

"And how they decide

ROBIN.

WOODPECKER.

where to stop and build their nests," said Mrs. Leonard.

"Very interesting questions, but no one has answered them yet," said Uncle Robert. "Migrating birds are all found in the south in winter, and we see them in the spring."

"What do you mean by mi-grat-ing birds?" asked Susie.

"Birds that fly from one part of the country to another," said Uncle Robert.

"The bluebird is the first to come," said Donald.

"A patch of blue sky," said Uncle Robert.

"You forget the geese that screech over our heads in the early spring," said Frank. "They fly in flocks shaped like an arrow."

"The 'bobwhite' is the funniest little bird. One comes right up to my garden fence. It is a shame to shoot them!" said Susie.

"It is a shame to kill any bird unless you need it for food. Every time a bird is killed the farmer loses one of his best helpers. The birds work for the farmer from morning to night."

"Oh, now you are making fun, Uncle Robert," said Susie. "The birds don't work at all. They just fly around and have a good time."

"The crows don't work for the farmer when they pull up his corn," said Frank.

Oriole.

"Nor the hawks when they steal his chickens," added Mr. Leonard.

"The cherry birds steal the cherries, and the sparrows eat the strawberries," said Susie.

"You would soon find out how much the birds do if they should all fly away," said Uncle Robert.

"The cankerworms would eat the leaves of the apple and other trees, and insects of all kinds would destroy the crops. The crow taxes the corn in payment for all the good he does. The hawks eat a thousand mice to one chicken—in fact, very few hawks eat chickens, anyway. The cherry birds and sparrows should be allowed a little toll for all the fruit they save. I want you to read a charming book called *The Great World's Farm*. The author calls birds 'Nature's militia.' The morning song of the birds means 'We are going to help the farmer to-day.'"

"That's true," said Mr. Leonard. "The farmers are just learning what a help the birds are to them. We have found that they eat the grubs, the worms, and the bugs before they eat everything else."

"Would there be very many more worms than there are now," asked Susie, "if the birds should go away?"

Bluebird.

CROW.

"You don't remember, do you, Susie," said her mother, "how many caterpillars there were in the village the year they tried to drive the sparrows away?"

"I do," said Donald. "Wasn't it dreadful? Why, Uncle Robert, the leaves were all eaten off the trees, and you could hardly take a step without squashing a caterpillar."

"Ugh!" said Susie with a shudder. "I'm glad I was too little to remember it."

"But the strange part of it was," said Frank, "that out here we hardly saw a caterpillar all summer."

"And our trees were never more beautiful," said Mrs. Leonard.

"Perhaps the village sparrows came to visit you," said Uncle Robert.

"They must have," said Donald. "The woods were full of them."

"I have read," said Uncle Robert, "that some small birds eat every day as much as their own weight in worms and insects."

"Oh, my!" said Susie. "I wonder how many worms that would be."

"The appetite of the small bird," said Mr. Leonard, looking at Donald with a smile, "must be something like that of a small boy."

They had now left the woods and were going toward the timothy meadow to get the painted cups. Donald was right.

One corner of the meadow was bright with the vivid red patches.

The sun was setting when they reached home. As they passed the woodpile in the back yard Donald said:

"I wonder how old that wood is! I'm going to see if I can count the rings."

"Show them to me, Donald," said Susie. "I never saw them."

Just then the clear, rich song of a bird rang out from the top of a tree on the edge of the woods.

"Hark!" said Mr. Leonard. "That is the thrush."

They listened until the song was ended.

"What a lovely walk we have had!" said Susie. "I'm not a bit tired. Are you, mother?"

"Well, a little," said Mrs. Leonard, "but we never had a more delightful afternoon. Thank you, dear," as Frank brought an easy-chair from the house to the porch for her. "Now I shall be rested in a few minutes."

"Let me put your flowers in water with mine, mother," said Susie.

"Tell Jane to bring our supper out here," said Mrs. Leonard. "It is too pleasant to go in the house."

"And tell her to be quick about it," said Donald. "I'm starving!"

"As hungry as a sparrow," said Uncle Robert, smiling.

While they were eating, the twilight came on.

"Listen!" whispered Frank, as a queer, clucking sound was heard among the bushes. Then came the cry:

"Whip-poor-will! whip-poor-will!"

"I wish I could see a whip-poor-will," said Donald. "They never let me get near enough to them to see how they look."

"Let's try this one," said Frank. "It's very near."

On tiptoe they slipped off the porch, but the shy bird heard them and flew away. Soon they heard it again:

"Whip-poor-will! whip-poor-will!"

And another one answered from the edge of the cornfield:

"Whip-poor-will! whip-poor-will!"

WHIP-POOR-WILL.

CHAPTER X

THE THUNDERSHOWER.

It had been growing warmer all day. When Susie looked at the thermometer at noon she wrote "82 degrees" in her little book. As they sat around the dinner table Uncle Robert asked:

"Do you find it hot in the meadow to-day?" "Rather warm," replied Mr. Leonard, "but it is fine haying weather. By night we shall have the hay in off that twenty acres, and it will be the finest crop of timothy I have had in years."

The haying had begun four days before. For a week Mr. Leonard had visited the field of timothy daily, and when he found the long heads of the graceful grass in full bloom he said:

"It is ready. We must begin to-morrow."

So the next morning the horses were hitched to the mowing machine, and Peter drove out to the meadow. The plumy heads of the tall timothy swayed on their slender stalks as they bowed before the breeze that swept over the meadow, making it look in the sunshine like the rippling surface of a quiet lake.

It seemed a pity to cut it down, but Peter thought only of the fine hay it would make, as he drove around the meadow again and again, each time coming nearer the center.

No sound broke the stillness but the "click, click" of the

MOWING THE MEADOW.

sharp knives, at the touch of which the tall grass quivered a moment and then fell.

In the afternoon Donald rode the rake, to which one of the horses, strong and steady, was hitched. The horse knew his business. He needed no direction from Donald as up and down the meadow he went, with slow and even steps.

Donald sat on the small round seat, his hand grasping the lever by which he raised and lowered the long curved teeth of the rake that gathered up the hay and dropped it in long rows called windrows.

Mr. Leonard and Frank followed with their pitchforks, and piled the windrows into big round cocks. The sun shone hot and clear. A strong, dry south wind was blowing, and the air was filled with the sweet smell of the newly mown hay.

The second day Mr. Leonard rode the machine while Peter and Frank opened the hay that had been cocked the day before, so that it would be nicely dried. By noon it was all cut.

The next day they raked it up for the last time and began to stow it away in the big haymows in the barn, where the very smell of it would make the horses hungry.

"Susie and I are coming out to help this afternoon," said Uncle Robert, as, after a short rest in the cool porch, the haymakers, started for the meadow again.

"We'll take all the help we can get," replied Mr. Leonard.

"I am afraid it is going to rain," said Uncle Robert, as he started a little later with Susie for the hayfield. "The barometer has fallen since morning."

"But, uncle," said Susie, "I don't see any clouds."

"Watch, and you'll see them before long," returned Uncle Robert. "What is that in the west now?"

RAKING AND COCKING HAY.

"It looks like the beginning of a cloud," said Susie.

Mr. Leonard, Peter, and Frank were loading the hay into a big wagon, while Donald raked after them.

"There's a shower coming," said Uncle Robert, pointing toward the west.

All paused and looked at the bank of clouds just coming into sight along the western horizon.

The air was still and sultry. Great beads of perspiration rolled down the faces of the haymakers.

"It's going to rain, sure," shouted Mr. Leonard, "and we must hurry or this fine hay will be spoiled. Harness up the horses to the other hayrack, Frank and Donald—be quick!"

The boys did not need urging. They felt the need, and ran to the barn.

"Bring some extra pitchforks!" shouted their father after them.

Uncle Robert pulled off his coat, and the spirit of his boyhood days came back.

Susie seized a rake and began to gather the scattered hay and pile it on the cocks.

The fresh span of horses galloped into the field. Frank brought them to a stand between two long rows of haycocks.

How they all worked! The very horses seemed to understand. They started with a jump to each new cock, and stood perfectly still as one after the other was added to their load.

"It is coming!" shouted Peter, swinging his fork to spread the great bundles of hay which came flying up to him.

The clouds looked like mountains with snowy peaks as they rose rapidly in the southwest. The mass moved under the sun and the bright silver color changed to blackness. Lightning flashes followed one another quickly. The low rumbling of thunder stirred the still air.

"It is coming!" cried Donald, as he took the reins to move to another cock. "G'long!"

All was hurry and excitement. Mrs. Leonard and Jane appeared on the scene with rakes in hand. Barri bounded from horse to horse as if that was some help.

Suddenly it grew darker. The leaves began to quiver. A curious light crept over the fields.

"There is the wind," shouted Frank. "The rain will be here in a minute."

Clouds completely covered the sky. Black forms seemed to dart out of their heavy masses.

"There's a drop," cried Susie.

Then what a wind! Straw hats were whirled away, but there was no time to run after them.

THE COMING STORM.

"Pile up the hay!"

The great loads staggered.

"Drive for the barn!" shouted Mr. Leonard. "Some of it must spoil, I suppose. We have done our best."

The horses moved off on the run, Frank's team ahead.

A roll and a crash of thunder followed a zigzag flash.

The hay was under cover, and the rain poured down.

They reached the porch just as it began to fall thick and fast. A moment more and it came down in floods, while at the same time the darkness passed away.

"How cool it is growing!" said Mrs. Leonard.

"It is twelve degrees cooler than it was at noon," said Donald, looking at the thermometer. "See, the wind has changed. It is from the northeast now."

Frank went into the dining-room, and when he came back he said, "The barometer has risen two-tenths of an inch since we looked at it last."

It seemed to rain harder than ever. The water was driven in sheets before the strong northeast wind. A stream began to run down the garden path. A vivid flash of lightning was followed quickly by a loud crash of thunder.

"That struck somewhere near," said Frank.

"I believe it was over in the wood," said Mrs. Leonard.

"See," said Uncle Robert in a few moments, pointing to a line of light in the western sky, "it is clearing already. The shower will soon be over."

The light in the west grew rapidly. The lightning became less frequent. The thunder rolled farther and farther away. The rain fell less and less heavily. The weather vane that had pointed to the northeast began to waver, and then turned toward the southwest again. It rained steadily but more gently as the clouds rolled away eastward.

And then the sun, lower now by two hours than when it was first hidden by the cloud, shone out clear and bright. Instantly everything glistened as with millions of diamonds. Even the air seemed to be filled with them, as though each raindrop was turned into a jewel as it fell.

Uncle Robert went to the front of the house and looked toward the dark cloud that was now piled up in the eastern sky.

"Come and see the rainbow!" he called.

As they looked at the bright and perfect arch that lay against the dark mass of clouds, Susie asked, "What makes rainbows, uncle?"

"It is the sun shining on the rain," replied Uncle Robert "This beautiful sunlight is made up of many, many rays. These rays fly from the sun as straight as arrows from a bow, unless something comes in their way to stop them. It seems as though such sharp little arrows of light would go right through raindrops. But they don't. They glance off the little round balls of water and bound up again like rubber balls.

"Now you know if you throw a ball straight down at your feet it bounds back into your hands. If you throw it from you, when it strikes the ground it bounds farther away. It is just so with these little arrows of light that we call rays. If the sun is high, as it is at noon, the rays are thrown back to it again. That is why we never have rainbows at noon. But when the sun is low, as it is now, instead of going back to the place they came from, they bound up against that cloud, and so make the wonderful rainbow."

"But, uncle," asked Donald, "why do we see so many colors in the rainbow? They are not in the sunlight."

"Oh, yes, they are," was the answer. "These rays of light are of the same colors that we see in the rainbow. It takes all of them mixed together to make the clear white light which we call sunlight, and without which nothing could live or grow.

"As the raindrops throw them up against that cloud, they are separated again, because some colors are more easily bent than others. The red, you see, is the highest and the violet the lowest in the bow. The raindrops make a prism. You have seen a prism. But through the prism the colors are turned the other way; the red is lowest and the violet highest."

"How fast the rainbow is fading away!" said Susie. "I wish it would stay."

"The rain is over," announced Donald, leaving them and walking out toward the garden. "The sky is quite clear."

"It is getting warm again," said Frank, looking at the thermometer, "but it does not feel hot as it did before the rain."

"The barometer is just where it was this morning," said Susie, coming from the dining-room.

"It is drying off very fast," said Uncle Robert. "Let us walk out and see how the garden stood its drenching."

"Put on your rubbers, Susie," called Mrs. Leonard from the house.

As they crossed the yard they passed a pan in the bottom of which the water stood an inch or more deep.

"That shows how much rain fell," said Uncle Robert, pointing to the pan.

"Do you mean if it had stayed on the ground where it fell it would have been that deep all over?" asked Susie. "Would that have been very much?"

"I think it would," was the smiling reply. "You might try to find out how much fell on the garden alone if it was an inch deep all over."

Susie shook her head.

"I don't know how," she said.

"Uncle," said Frank, "in the weather reports they always tell how much rain falls, even if it is only a small part of an inch. How can they tell when it is so little?"

"They have what is called a rain gauge, by which a very small amount of rainfall can be measured. By the way, we might have a rain-gauge of our own. It would be easy to make one with the help of a tinsmith. Is there a tinsmith in the village?"

"Yes," answered Frank, "but I don't believe he has much to do."

"So much the better for us," laughed Uncle Robert. "Susie, while these other people are busy tomorrow, shall we drive to the village and see if we can get the tinsmith to help us make a rain-gauge? I have a little book somewhere that tells just how it should be done."

Susie was delighted at the thought of such a day with Uncle Robert, and the boys were so interested in the prospect of having a rain-gauge of their own that they could hardly wait for to-morrow to come.

CHAPTER XI.

THE VILLAGE.

The next morning Frank harnessed Nell for Uncle Robert and Susie to drive into the village to see the tinsmith.

It was a delightful ride through the woods and the fields washed clean by the rain. The birds were singing gayly. The air was fresh and clear. Long shadows lay along the road.

The tinsmith was sitting by his open door, tilted back in an old wooden chair. As Nell stopped, he brought his chair down on its four legs and said:

"Good morning."

Uncle Robert lifted Susie out of the wagon and hitched Nell to a post. The tinsmith rose to his feet, smiling to Susie, who said:

"This is my Uncle Robert, Mr. Mills. We've come to have a rain-gauge made."

"Good morning," said Uncle Robert, turning to Mr. Mills, who looked as if he thought rain gauges were not exactly in his line. "Can you spare us a little time this morning? Susie must have her rain-gauge before the next shower."

"Come right in," said Mr. Mills, "and tell me what your rain-gauge looks like. I never heard of such a thing."

With Uncle Robert's careful direction he soon understood

The village street.

what they wanted. They saw him well started in the work, and then Uncle Robert said:

"Come, Susie, let's go to the post office.—How long before the rain-gauge will be finished?" he asked of Mr. Mills. "Shall we have time to get dinner?"

"I think I can have it ready by two o'clock," answered Mr. Mills.

"Then we'll take Nell to the hotel," said Uncle Robert.

They drove slowly under the big cottonwood trees which shaded the street.

"Isn't it nice that it takes such a long time to make a rain-gauge?" said Susie. "Here we are at the hotel now, Uncle Robert. It's such a little way."

From the hotel they strolled to the store, the center of life and interest in the village.

One corner of the store was taken up by the post office. Back from that ran long lines of shelves which reached to the ceiling. Beneath them were bins for flour and sugar. On the lower shelves were canisters of tea, coffee, and spices, and glass candy jars, which looked very inviting to Susie. Some were filled with gay-striped sticks. There were also jars of peppermint lozenges, star—and heart-shaped, with pink mottoes on their white faces.

On the upper shelves were rows upon rows of cans covered with gay pictures of fruits and vegetables.

Opposite the groceries were long shelves of dry goods. A glass case at one end of the counter was filled with bright-colored ribbons.

In the darkness at the back of the store stood the barrels of vinegar, molasses, and kerosene oil. Above them hung rows of well-cured hams and sides of bacon. Near the barrels stood an old rusty stove which bore the marks of long use.

Uncle Robert asked for the mail. Susie looked longingly at the glass jars upon the shelf, trusting that Uncle Robert would understand her even if she didn't say anything.

"We must have some candy," he said. "Tell Mr. Jenkins what you would like, Susie, while I look at my letters."

Susie carefully picked out three sticks of peppermint, three sticks of lemon, and three of cinnamon.

"If you please, I'd like some of the mottoes, too."

Mr. Jenkins handed down the jar, spread out a clean sheet of wrapping paper, and turned out the candies.

Susie selected a dozen hearts, rounds, and stars, with different mottoes, and then wondered if she ought to have lemon drops, too.

"Do you think I have enough, uncle?" she asked.

Uncle Robert knew pretty well what little girls like.

"No, Susie," he said, "you have forgotten the lemon drops, and, let me see, nut candy—we must carry home enough for mother and the boys."

Just then a little girl in a pink sunbonnet, carrying an oil can in her hand, came through the open door.

"How d' do, Susie," she said, with a shy glance at Uncle Robert.

"How d' do," said Susie. "Have some of my candy, Jennie?" holding it out to her. "Uncle Robert bought it for me. There he is," in a loud whisper.

"Good morning, Jennie," said Uncle Robert, putting his letters in his pocket. "You haven't been out to see Susie since I have been here."

"It's Jennie's mother who had the nasturtiums last year," said Susie. "Have you any now Jennie?"

"Yes, but they don't grow well this year," answered Jennie.

"Perhaps you need new seeds," said Uncle Robert. "They are apt to do better if they are raised on different soil."

"I have some nasturtiums this year, Jennie," said Susie. "They are just beginning to blossom. I'll save you some seed if you want me to."

"Come out some day and see Susie's flowers, Jennie," said Uncle Robert kindly, as they left the store.

"Good-by, Jennie," said Susie.

"Time for dinner," said Uncle Robert. "I'm hungry."

Susie's eyes danced.

They went into the dining-room and sat down at the long table. Through the window they could see the hotel garden from which the flowers on the table had been gathered.

"What shall we do now?" asked Uncle Robert as, after dinner, they stood upon the porch, looking up and down the street.

No sound was heard but the sleepy noonday song of the grasshopper and the occasional rattle of a wagon going down to the store.

"Let's go to the mill," said Susie.

"The mill wasn't running when we passed there this morning," said Uncle Robert. "Suppose we wait until some time when the boys are with us. Then we can go all through it, and see just how wheat is changed into flour."

"Oh, yes," said Susie, "that will be the nicest."

"We might go to the station and see the train come in," suggested Uncle Robert, looking at his watch.

"Oh, that's fun! Come on, uncle," cried Susie, running down the steps. "See, they are all going down now!"

"All right," said Uncle Robert, "but don't hurry; there's plenty of time."

As they looked down the track they could see the steel rails

A FREIGHT TRAIN.

gleaming in the hot sunshine. The two shining lines stretched away until they seemed to meet in the distance.

In the other direction a faint line of smoke appeared over the trees. It grew more and more distinct, until at last an engine rounded the curve and came puffing heavily up the track, pulling a long line of cars behind it.

"That's a freight train," said Uncle Robert.

"It stops here to let the passenger go by," said the station master, who stood near. "Expecting some one to-day, sir? The train isn't due for ten minutes."

"Not to-day," replied Uncle Robert. "Do many trains stop here?"

"Not many," said the station master as he hurried away to the switch.

The great engine, drawing its heavy load after it, turned into the side track. When the small caboose at the end had passed the switch a man, who was running upon the tops of the cars, waved his arms and the long line stood still.

"The engine breathes hard—just like Barri after a long run," said Susie. "I wonder what is in all these cars, uncle."

"Here is one marked 'Furniture,' from a large factory in Grand Rapids," said Uncle Robert, reading the white card that was tacked on the side. "It is going to a town in Nebraska."

"What funny cars these open ones are!" said Susie; "the ones with the shelves in. What are they for? They're empty, too. I shouldn't think they'd want to drag empty cars about."

"These are the cars poultry is shipped in," explained Uncle Robert. "Perhaps they have been to Chicago with chickens for the market, and are on the way back to the place they came from for more."

"How many of these big yellow cars there are!" said Susie. "They all have re-frig-re-frig—"

"Refrigerator," prompted Uncle Robert.

"Oh, I know what a refrigerator is," said Susie. "It's an ice box. Are these cars ice boxes, uncle?"

"Yes; the great packing houses at the stock yards in Chicago ship beef all over the country in them. The fruit from California comes in refrigerator cars, too."

"There's the train!" cried Susie, "and here comes Mr. Jenkins with the mail."

The train came rushing on. Susie thought it was not going to stop. But suddenly it slowed up. The conductor leaped upon the platform. The train stood still. Heads were thrust out of the windows. A few passengers alighted. Brakemen ran along the platform.

"All aboard!" shouted the conductor, waving his hand to

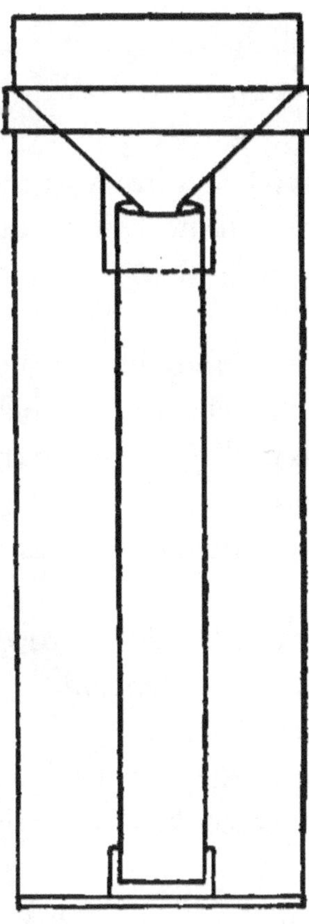

RAIN-GAUGE.

the engineer, who was leaning out of the cab window watching for the signal.

"Ding-dong, ding-dong, puff, puff, toot, toot," and the train was off.

"Now we'll go and see if there is any mail for us," said Uncle Robert. "Then we'll go to the tinsmith's."

The rain-gauge was just finished. So Susie waited in the shop while Uncle Robert went to the stable for Nell, who pricked up her ears when she saw him. She was beginning to think she had been forgotten.

It was late in the afternoon when they reached home. Mrs. Leonard and the boys were looking for them when they drove in at the gate.

It took some time to choose just the right place for the rain-gauge, but at last they decided upon a little rise of ground that lay between the house and the orchard.

There was first the funnel-shaped receiver, one and one-half inches deep and eight inches in diameter. Below this was a tube two and five-tenths inches in diameter and twenty inches long. At the top of this tube, close to the receiver, there was a small hole.

"What is that hole for?" asked Donald.

"So if it rains more than enough to fill this tube," explained Susie, who knew all about it, "it can run out of the hole."

"Then it will be lost," said Donald.

"No," replied Uncle Robert, "it is to be set inside of this cylinder, which is twenty-three and one-half inches long, but only six inches in diameter, and so is smaller than the top of the receiver.

"The water that runs from that hole falls into this. By measuring it in the small tube, and adding it to what the tube held before, we can know how much there is in all. One inch in the tube would be one-tenth of an inch in the receiver."

"Then twenty inches, or the tube full, would be two inches in the receiver," said Frank.

"Yes," said his uncle; "but how shall we make this stand up?"

"We might pile stones around it," suggested Donald.

"That will be a good way," said Uncle Robert. There were some stones in a pile near the orchard fence. Frank and Donald picked them up and placed them about the rain-gauge until it stood firm.

"Well, these stones are of some use after all," said Frank.

"I'm glad of it," said Donald. "It seemed as though we should never get them all picked up. I believe stones grow."

"These stones tell a wonderful story," said Uncle Robert, smiling.

"Oh, uncle, when are you going to tell it to us? To-night?" asked Susie.

"Not to-night, my dear. You have had stories enough for one day," and Uncle Robert took her by the hand and started for the house.

"We have a regular weather bureau of our own now," said Donald. "I hope it will rain all day long to-morrow."

CHAPTER XII

A DAY ON THE RIVER.

"Father, can't we have a picnic on the river?" asked Susie.

"Please, do let us have a picnic," said Donald.

"I think you may," said Mr. Leonard. "You might have it to-morrow. I won't need the boys."

"Hurrah!" cried Donald, and Susie skipped and danced for joy.

"We'll have to have a nice lunch," said Frank.

"What shall it be?" asked Mrs. Leonard.

"Oh, we can take some ham sandwiches—"

"And some cake and jelly," put in Susie.

"And some cold chicken and boiled eggs," added Donald.

"Oh," cried Susie, "let us take our eggs along all fresh and boil them! We can take a little pail and—"

"I'll tell you what we'll do," interrupted Frank. "We'll take some salt pork, and catch some fish, and have a fry."

Frank looked at the barometer and said it was going to be a nice day. The sun was setting clear and bright. The children went to bed happy and dreamed of the fun to-morrow.

In the morning Susie rushed out to see if it was good weather. The sun was shining brightly, and she turned and looked at her long shadow that reached clear over the barn. The direction of the shadow was southwest.

Donald took a tin can and went out into one corner of the garden, where the soil was dark, rich, and damp, and with a shovel dug up great mud worms, and almost filled his can.

Frank got out two cane poles, rigged the lines and hooks, and put on the sinkers.

"I want to catch a fish," said Susie.

"All right," said Frank; "we'll cut a pole for you when we get on the island. We shall not fish till we get there."

Uncle Robert watched the enthusiasm of the children with a pleasant smile. Mrs. Leonard and Susie put up the lunch.

"Put in a paper of salt for the fish, please," called Frank.

"Don't believe you will catch many fish," said Mr. Leonard. "You know the last time you went you didn't catch any."

"It is not a good day for fish," said Uncle Robert; "it is too bright."

"We'll get some sunfish, anyway," said Donald, "and perhaps we shall catch a perch or two and a catfish."

At last all was ready Frank took the oars from the beams of the shed, Uncle Robert carried the big basket, Donald followed with the fish poles and the can of worms, while Susie brought up the rear with a small tin bucket.

Away they went, down the slope and over the bottom land to the mouth of the creek, where the boat was moored. Soon they glided out from the shore under Frank's steady stroke.

"We will go up on this side, where it is easier to row," he said. "The current is on the other side next to the bank."

"Why do you suppose the current is over there?" asked Uncle Robert.

"I don't know," said Frank. "Last spring we had a big flood, and the current was so strong that it took away a lot of earth from that bank. The earth fell down into the river and was carried away. Mr. Davis lost a good deal of land."

"Tell me about the flood, Frank," said Uncle Robert.

"Last March the ice broke up in the river and went tearing downstream in great blocks," began Frank. "Just below the dam, between the island and that shore," pointing to the woods, "it piled up until there was a big ice jam. You could cross over to the island on foot. Then the water began to rise until it was nearly even with the top of the dam. At first it went round close to the ridge. You see the land is lower there. The part of our cornfield next to the river was an island. Then the water rose higher, and spread all over the bottom land. It made the mouth of the creek close to the slope, and the water came up around the trunks of the trees.

"On the other side, where the current is, it didn't get over the bank, but it tore away lots of earth. Three big trees fell into the water and were carried down the river. Ever so many trees came down. Peter and I caught a lot and piled them up for firewood."

"Don't you remember, Frank," said Susie, "two or three sheds came down, too?"

"The miller thought it would carry away the mill," said Donald.

"The water looks pretty clear now. How did it look then?" asked Uncle Robert.

"At first it was clear," said Frank. "Then it got just like coffee."

"That was the dirt in the water," said Donald.

"When the water went down," continued Frank, "the bottom land was all covered with the stuff the river left. Father says the dirt it brought makes the land better."

"What do you suppose made the freshet?" asked Uncle Robert.

"Oh, they said it was the snow melting, away up the river," answered Donald. "The snow was gone here, but we had lots of rain."

"Where is the deepest part of the river?" asked Uncle Robert.

"It is quite deep on the other side," said Frank, "but it is shallow over here. Farther down it is deeper in the middle."

"Where is the current down there?" asked Uncle Robert.

"In the middle of the river," said Frank.

"When we go in swimming we can wade out here a long ways before we go over our heads," said Donald.

"I wish I could swim," said Susie.

"You should learn," said Uncle Robert. "The boys could easily teach you."

They rowed steadily up the river. At last they reached the island and landed. It was long and narrow, covered with trees and green grass. Here and there low bushes grew down to the water's edge, while at the upper end there were many boulders, stones, pebbles, and clean white sand.

A STRING OF FISH.

They brought up the basket and put it in a cool place under a tree.

"Now for the fishing!" said Frank.

Up the river they could see the dam, and on the left of the dam the flour mill.

"There is a nice big pond up above the dam," said Susie. "We ought to go up there some day."

"I think it is better fishing there," said Frank, "but we would have to drag the boat around the dam."

Uncle Robert stretched himself under the shade of an elm tree. Susie rolled up her sack and put it under his head. The boys went off to try their luck at fishing. They cut a pole for Susie, but she soon tired of sitting still, and came back to pick up sticks for the fire so that everything would be ready to fry the fish.

When the boys came back they brought three little sunfish, two perch, and one funny-looking fish with horns, which Frank said was a catfish.

Frank and Uncle Robert dressed the fish, while Donald rowed across the river to a place where he knew there was a spring, and soon returned with a pail of clear, sparkling water.

Susie spread the cloth in a nice shady place, and unpacked the basket. The eggs were boiled in the tin bucket over the fire. Frank fried the fish, and at last dinner was ready.

"Oh, isn't this fun!" said Susie.

"Grand!" said Frank.

"I'd like to be an Indian and live in the woods all the time," said Donald.

"We could make a fort," said Frank, "on that bank of the island and mount cannon, and not allow any ships to come up the river."

"Oho!" laughed Donald. "Ships don't come up this river. The water isn't deep enough."

"That doesn't matter," said Susie; "we could play they do."

After the luncheon was over and the basket packed again they sat about under the trees.

"What a good view of the dam there is from here!" said Uncle Robert.

"I know why they built the dam there," said Frank. "Just above the dam the water was quite swift."

"What makes the water swift?" asked Donald.

"Because the bed of the river slopes more there than down here," said Uncle Robert; "and in places on rivers where there are rapids they build dams in order to use the water for the mills."

"Oh, yes, I know how they use the water," said Donald. "They have a sluice, and they lift the gate, and the water comes through, and that turns the mill wheels."

"In some rivers there are ponds larger than that pond up there, where there are no dams," said Uncle Robert.

"Yes," said Frank, "there is a little lake down the river. We will go there some day. It is good fishing. How much better our corn looks than the corn on that hill over there! I tell you, it takes bottom land like ours to raise good corn."

"What makes the corn such a beautiful green?" asked Susie.

"That is quite a question," said Uncle Robert. "We will try and find out some day. But I want to know what makes the bottom land richer than the land up on the prairie?"

"Well," said Frank slowly, "I suppose that the dirt brought down by the river and spread out over it makes it richer."

"Where does that dirt come from?"

THE MILL AND DAM.

"Way up the river."

"If I should call the bottom land a flood-plain," said Uncle Robert, "would you know why?"

"Oh, I know," said Donald. "Because the water covers it when there is a flood."

"Now what made that flood-plain?"

"Wasn't it always there?"

"No," said Uncle Robert. "The river made it."

"How could the river make the flood-plain?" asked Susie.

"Why, you told me a moment ago that the river brought down great quantities of dirt and left it all along the shores," said Uncle Robert.

"But it wouldn't bring down enough to make all that field, would it?" asked Donald.

"The river is a great worker," said Uncle Robert. "It is

at work now, and has been working for many, many long years. It has not only made this flood-plain, but many others. Sometimes the river carries this dirt clear out into the sea, and sometimes it piles it up at its mouth so that a delta is formed."

"Oh, yes," said Donald, "we studied about that in geography when we had school, but I didn't know a delta was made that way."

"Are there any deltas in this part of the river?" asked Susie.

"There may be," replied Uncle Robert, "wherever one stream flows into another."

"Is there one at the mouth of our creek?" asked Frank.

"We will look when we go back," replied Uncle Robert. "Shall we take a walk now?"

When they reached the upper end of the island they sat down on some large boulders that formed part of the tiny beach. Just above them was the flood of water pouring over the dam. The bright sunshine made the foam look white and glistening, lighted here and there with colors of the rainbow.

The water rumbled and roared as it rushed out of the mill pond. To the left were the flour mill and the village. They could hear the mill wheel turning. They could see a little white church half hidden among the trees.

A kingfisher swept by them with a voice like a watchman's rattle.

"He knows how to catch fish better than we do," said Donald.

Susie picked up some pebbles and put them in her apron. She tried to get a number of colors. Some were nearly red, some were blue, and some were white.

"Can you find one that is exactly round?" asked Uncle Robert.

"Here's a white one that's almost round," and Susie held up a quartz pebble.

"Where do you suppose this little white pebble came from?" asked Uncle Robert.

"Did it come from away up the river—a long way?" said Donald.

"I think so. One day this pebble was a part of some rock or quarry. How it was broken off, how it came down, how it was made round, is well worth studying."

"Oh, tell us about it, please," begged Susie.

"We'll read about it together," said Uncle Robert, "in the Big Book."

"What book?" asked Donald.

"The book that lies all around us, which was written by the Creator of the world," said Uncle Robert. "We are reading a page of it now."

"Just under the current out there," said Frank, "the bed of the river is covered with all kinds of stones. Some of them are as big as these boulders. I suppose the river brought them down."

"What do you think makes the pebbles round?" asked Uncle Robert.

"Maybe the river wears off the rough edges," suggested Frank, thoughtfully.

"Yes," said Uncle Robert, "the current of the river rolls them over and over on the river bed, and they rub and grind against each other."

"What becomes of the stuff that is worn off from them?" asked Frank.

"Don't you see it—there?" said Uncle Robert, pointing to the beach.

"Oh, you mean the sand," said Donald, taking up a handful and examining it.

"Is that the way the nice white sand is made?" asked Susie.

"That's what you meant when you said the river worked," said Frank. "Did these boulders come down the river too?"

"The story of the boulders," said Uncle Robert, "is different from the story of the pebbles. The water helped grind the pebbles, but it took ice to make the boulders."

"Ice!" the children all exclaimed.

"Yes, ice. A long, long while ago this land was covered by a great river, or sea of ice, and that was the time these boulders were made," said Uncle Robert.

"Can we read about that in the Big Book?" asked Donald.

"Some of it," said Uncle Robert. "There are many wonderful stories in this beautiful world—stories more wonderful than any fairy tale. But we must go home now, children; it's getting late."

The setting sun threw long shadows of the trees over the river as they rowed home, and the happy day was done.

CHAPTER XIII.

A RAINY DAY.

It was raining, but no one was surprised. They had expected it.

The day before had been one of those warm, midsummer days, beginning with a clear sky and a strong south wind. By noon heavy white clouds that looked like heaps of down floated slowly overhead.

The weather vane, which in the morning had pointed to the south, turned from side to side, as though uncertain which direction it liked best. Toward afternoon it seemed to settle the question in favor of the east.

THE WEATHER VANE.

The clouds did not rise higher and become thinner and more scattered, as such clouds do if the weather is fair. They kept their white, billowy edges, and rested heavily on straight bands of dull gray.

When the sun set, the scroll—like edges of the clouds were tinged with gold and rose color, but under the glittering fringe remained the solid banks of gray and misty purple.

The thermometer had been high all day, for it was very warm. The barometer had slowly but surely fallen.

Then, too, the Weather Report, just received, told of a storm that had started in the southwestern part of the country and was moving northeast. Uncle Robert had said, at the rate it was traveling, it might reach them some time the next day.

And now it was raining in a quiet, steady way. The clouds had lost their billowy whiteness. They were one dull, heavy, unbroken mass of gray. The wind blew steadily from the southeast.

A rainy day was before them.

"The very thing we need," said Mr. Leonard. "The corn is just ready for it, and the pastures are beginning to look pretty dry."

"Let's go fishing, Don," said Frank. "I'll go and dig some worms while you get the lines ready."

"Say we do," said Donald, starting off at once.

"Do you want some company, boys?" asked Uncle Robert, smiling.

"You bet-ter believe!" said Donald, catching himself just in time.

"Hurrah for the rainy day!" cried Frank as he pulled on his rubber boots and coat and went out to dig the worms.

"Shall we take the boat?" asked Uncle Robert.

"Oh, yes," said Donald. "I'll get the oars."

"We'll have fish for dinner to-day, mother," said Frank.

"Be sure you come back in time, then," said Mrs. Leonard, smiling.

"I wish I was a boy and could go fishing in the rain," said Susie as she watched them start off.

Down the hill they went, and Susie, watching them from the front porch, saw them push the boat from the landing and throw out their lines as they drifted down the stream. Then the trees hid them from sight.

It was dinner time when they returned.

"I told you we'd have fish to-day," said Frank triumphantly, holding up a string of bass and perch.

"You boys will have to clean them," said Mrs. Leonard. "Jane is ready to cook them now."

"Come on, Don," called Frank. "My, won't they be good!"

In the afternoon it ceased to rain. It became lighter and the clouds looked higher and thinner.

"It's going to clear off," said Susie, going to the window.

"I wonder how much rain has fallen," said Uncle Robert.

"I'm going to look at the rain-gauge," said Frank.

"I'll go too," said Donald.

When they came back they said there were fifteen inches of water in the measuring tube, which, in the receiver, would be an inch and a half.

"That would just fill it," said Donald.

"Does that mean," asked Susie, "that if the rain had stayed on the ground it would be an inch and a half deep all over?"

"Yes," answered Uncle Robert.

"Would that be very much?" she asked, taking the rod by which the rain in the gauge was measured and finding the mark for an inch and a half.

"We might find out how much it would be on Susie's garden," said Uncle Robert. "Does any one know how large the garden is?"

No one knew.

"Let's get father's tapeline and measure it," said Frank.

"Oh, do," said Susie, always interested in anything about her garden.

When they came in Donald said:

"It is muddy, but it's beginning to dry off in some places already."

"How big is the garden?" asked Susie.

"It is forty feet one way," said Frank, "and twenty-five feet the other."

"Take your paper and pencil, Frank," said Uncle Robert, "and draw a plan of it. You might make one inch for every ten feet, and see how that will come out."

Frank took the paper, pencil, and ruler, and soon he said:

"It makes it four inches long and two inches and a half wide."

"But remember," said Uncle Robert, "that means forty feet long and twenty-five feet wide."

"I'll write it down," said Frank; "then we'll remember."

So he wrote "40" on the long side and "25" on the short one.

"But we must find out how many square feet there are on the whole surface," said Uncle Robert.

"Well," said Frank, "there are forty this way."

"So we might think of it as a row across the garden of forty square feet, might we not?" suggested Uncle Robert.

"Yes," said Frank; "and if we do that there will be twenty-five rows just like it, won't there?"

"Exactly," said Uncle Robert. "How many does that make in all?"

"Twenty-five forties," said Frank, pencil in hand. "Why, that's just one thousand."

"That sounds pretty big," said Susie.

"Especially when you think of the weeds," said Uncle Robert, smiling, "How many square inches would that be, Frank?"

"Well," said Frank, "a foot is twelve inches long, and if it is square it is twelve inches wide, too."

"Then," said Uncle Robert, "if you call them rows of twelve square inches, how many rows would there be?"

"Why, twelve," said Donald.

"And so it would be—"

"One hundred forty-four," said Frank.

"Then," said Uncle Robert, "if there are one hundred forty-four square inches in one foot, how many in one thousand feet?"

"One hundred forty-four thousand," said Frank, after a moment's thought.

"But the rain-gauge says that an inch and a half of rain has fallen," said Uncle Robert, "and when an inch is as deep as it is long and broad, it is called a cubic inch. How much would one and one-half cubic inches be?"

"If this is one inch," said Frank, looking at the paper, "half an inch deep would be half of this, and that, added to this, would be an inch and a half. Isn't that right?"

He went to work again, and after a few minutes' silence he said:

"It makes two hundred and sixteen thousand inches in all."

"What kind of inches did we call them, Donald?"

"Cubic inches," said Donald.

"If you were to bring a pail of water from the spring," said Uncle Robert, "would you say you had so many inches of water?"

"No," said Frank, "it would be quarts, or gallons, or something like that."

"Do you know how much a quart or gallon is, Susie?" asked Uncle Robert.

"Mother has a quart cup in the pantry," said Susie, "that she measures the milk in sometimes, but I don't know how much a gallon is."

"My new milk pail," said Mrs. Leonard, who sat beside the window sewing, "holds just two gallons."

"Let's see how many quarts it takes to fill it," said Susie.

So they went into the kitchen, and Susie dipped the water with the quart cup into the tin pail.

"Eight," she said, when the pail would hold no more.

"If the pail holds two gallons, Susie." said Uncle Robert, "how many quarts are there in one gallon?"

"Four," said Susie, counting on her fingers.

"Well," said Uncle Robert as they went back into the dining-room, "now we have found how many quarts there are in a gallon; how shall we find how many gallons two hundred and sixteen thousand cubic inches will make?"

"If I knew how many cubic inches there are in one gallon," said Frank, "I could do it."

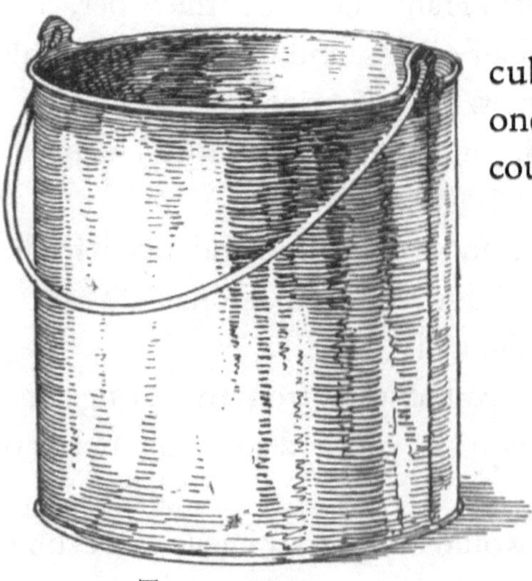

Two Gallons

One quart.

"How shall we find out?" asked Uncle Robert.

"We might measure a gallon," said Donald, "and then if we could empty it into a flat pan couldn't we measure that?"

"We can try," said Uncle Robert, "if your mother has the pan."

"You may use one of those tins I bake biscuit in," said Mrs. Leonard.

"I'll get it," said Susie.

They measured it and found it was eleven inches long, seven inches wide, and two inches deep. The gallon of water filled it one and one half time.

"If it had been three inches deep," said Frank, "the water would have just filled it."

"Well," said Uncle Robert, "can you find out how many inches there are in all?"

It took some time and several suggestions from Uncle Robert, but at last they found it to be two hundred thirty-one cubic inches.

"Now," said Uncle Robert, "can you find how many two hundred thirty-one cubic inches there are in two hundred and sixteen thousand cubic inches?"

"I know how," said Frank, figuring rapidly.

In a short time he found that two hundred and sixteen thousand cubic inches would make over nine hundred thirty-five gallons.

"If you were going to water the garden with the new two-gallon pail," said Uncle Robert, "how many times would you have to fill it?"

"If we took two gallons at a time," said Frank, "it would be—wait a minute—it would be four hundred sixty-seven and one half."

"My," said Donald, "it makes my arms ache to think of it."

"I'm going to find out how much fell on the whole farm some time," said Frank, "but I'm just tired out now."

"Where does all the rain come from?" asked Susie. "I don't see how so much water can stay in the clouds."

"It doesn't," said Donald, laughing. "That's why it rains."

"But where does it all go to?" asked Uncle Robert.

"Oh," said Susie, "it just goes into the ground."

"Some of it runs off into the river," said Donald. "That's what makes it rise when it rains hard."

"I wonder if it has risen much to-day?" said Frank.

"We might put on our rubber boots and walk down and see," said Uncle Robert. "It is clearing off finely."

"It is almost supper time now," said Mrs. Leonard. "If you'll wait I'll help Jane get it ready, and then you can go as soon as it is over."

So they waited, and by the time they started the sun was shining brightly. It would be a whole hour before it would set.

CHAPTER XIV.

THE WALK AFTER THE RAIN.

The sky was clear and bright as if it had been washed by the rain. The trees took on a fresher green. The corn held up its tasseled heads as if conscious of the strength the clouds had given it. The birds, too, rejoiced as they flew from tree to tree, singing their sweetest songs.

"How nice it is to get out after being in the house all day," said Susie, skipping along by Uncle Robert's side. "See that lovely blue sky. I wish I had a dress for my doll just that color."

"And when we came out this morning," said Uncle Robert, "Donald thought the clouds looked as though they were solid and could never break away."

"They're all gone now," said Donald. "I wonder where they went. Aren't the clouds lovely sometimes, uncle? I love to watch them when they look like great piles of snow."

"Yes," replied Uncle Robert, "when I was a boy I used to lie for hours under an old apple tree and watch the clouds. I fancied they had very wonderful forms, sometimes giants and dragons and all kinds of animals."

"You can see things in them," said Donald. "I often do."

"What are clouds made of, uncle?" asked Susie. "I wish I could get close to one and see what it is like."

THE CLOUDS.

"When people go up in balloons," said Donald, "they go through clouds sometimes."

"Have you never been in a cloud?" asked Uncle Robert, smiling.

"Oh, no," said Susie. "How could I? I've never been up in a balloon."

"I know," was the reply, "but have you never seen anything near the ground that looked at all like a cloud?"

"I don't remember," said Susie, shaking her head.

"We've seen fogs along the river," said Frank. "They

look a little like clouds. You know we see them almost every morning."

"Oh, yes," exclaimed Donald. "Don't you remember that fog we had early last spring? Why, uncle, it was so thick we couldn't see the barn from the house."

"And, uncle," said Susie, "I went out to the barn with father, and in a few minutes there were little drops of water on my hair, and all over my cloak."

"Did it last all day?" asked Uncle Robert.

"Oh, no," said Frank, "only for a little while in the morning. Then it went away and the sun came out."

THE GULLY.

"How did it go away?" asked Uncle Robert.

"Why," said Donald, "at first it began to get lighter, and we could see things plainer."

"And then," chimed in Susie, "it looked as though the fog broke up into pieces that rolled up in the sky, and floated off just like clouds."

"But what is that we see over the bottom land yonder?"

"It looks like fog," said Frank.

"More like steam, I think," said Donald.

"If it was up there against that blue sky instead of on the ground—" said Uncle Robert.

"Then it would be a cloud," said Susie. "Why, I never thought of that."

They had gone through the gate in front of the house, and were following the path that led down the slope to the spring.

"See how the water has plowed through the ground," said Frank, pointing to a gully the rain had made in the path.

"It took a good many rains to make that gully," said Donald.

"There was a little creek here for a while," said Frank. "The water has all run off now, but it has spoiled the path."

"Will the gully get deeper every time it rains?" asked Susie.

"Of course," said Donald. "That's what makes it."

"Why does the water run along the path?" asked Uncle Robert.

"Because it is lower than the ground on each side," said Frank.

"How deep do you think the water will dig into the path if we do not fill it up?" asked Uncle Robert.

"Oh, way, way down. I suppose," said Donald.

"But if grass grew on the path," said Frank, "the water wouldn't wear the ground away. We will have to fill it up with stones."

"See these pebbles, uncle," said Susie. "How did they get here? They look just like those we saw on the island."

"Do you remember what I told you about the boulders on the island?"

"Yes, you said the boulders were made by ice," answered Susie. "Did the ice make these pebbles?"

"Perhaps so, and perhaps the river made them and left them here."

"What! that river away down there? How could it get up here?"

"That river away down there once flowed right over this ground," said Uncle Robert. "This slope," pointing just above, "was its bank, and the ground under our feet its bed."

"That must have been a hundred years ago," said Donald.

"Yes, a great many hundred years ago. You see the work this bit of a stream has done in the path? Many rivers begin just this way. They are cutting and changing the earth all the time."

They had now come to the spring nearly at the foot of the slope. On sultry summer days it was a cool, inviting spot. The low-spreading branches of a beautiful bur oak shaded the little stream where it gushed from the outcropping limestone.

THE SPRING.

"Do you want a drink?" asked Susie, taking the tin dipper which always hung by the spring.

"Thank you, dear. How cool it is! It makes me think of the old spring in the hayfield where I used to work when I was a boy."

"The rain has not made the spring run any faster," said Donald.

"Where does this water come from?" asked Uncle Robert.

"From out of the ground," said Susie.

"How does it get into the ground?"

"It's always there, isn't it?" said Susie. "The spring runs all the time. I fill my pail here every day in the summer."

"Yes, don't you remember when the wells all dried up last summer," said Frank, "that the spring was all right?"

"Well, then, where has the water gone that fell to-day?" asked Uncle Robert.

"Most of it has run off into the creek and river," said Donald. "It would look just like a lake if it was an inch and a half deep all over the ground."

"Some of it has soaked into the ground," said Frank.

"How deep down into the ground?" asked Uncle Robert.

"Down to China," laughed Donald.

"How deep do you have to dig to find water—to China?"

"Our wells are about thirty feet deep," said Frank. "In a dry time there's no water in them."

"How is it when you have a long wet spell?"

"They are more than half full then."

"Have both wells the same depth?"

"I think so."

"Where does the water in the wells come from?"

"It is the rain that has soaked into the ground," said Frank.

"How far down does it go?"

"It must go down till it finds some hard clay or rock that stops it," said Frank.

"What does it do then?"

"Then," said Frank slowly, "it must go along on top of the rock or clay."

"When does it come out of the ground?"

"Oh, I see! The rain goes down until it comes to that lime

SECTION OF HILLSIDE.

rock. Then it goes along the rock, and comes out there," said Donald, pointing to the spring.

"Does it always?" asked Frank. "I have read of very deep wells that are bored down into the ground more than a thousand feet, and when the augur strikes water the water comes right up to the top of the ground."

"You are talking about artesian wells," said Uncle Robert.

"Yes, that is the name."

They had left the spring and were walking down toward the mouth of the creek. The rain had swollen the little stream, and the water was dark with dirt.

"See how muddy the water is," said Susie.

"The creek must bring down a lot of earth," said Frank.

"There are Joe and Dick Davis," said Donald, pointing across the river. "I wonder what they are doing? I'm going to see."

Donald ran along to the mouth of the creek, which he reached as the Davis boys began to scramble down the steep bank to the edge of the river.

"Hello there!" called Donald. "What are you fellows doing?"

"Sticking in the mud," replied Joe Davis, holding up first one foot and then the other, heavy with the stiff clay that hung to it.

"Why don't they go around by the path?" said Susie, coming up with Frank and Uncle Robert.

"They'll always take the short cut if there is one," laughed Frank. "Come along over here!" he shouted.

"All right," sang out Dick, scraping the mud from his shoes.

An eddy in the stream just above the steep bank made a quiet place in the current. Here their boat was moored. As they pushed out from the shore they were swept down the stream, but a few strong pulls carried them beyond the swiftest part of the current, and then they easily rowed back to the landing at the mouth of the creek, where the Leonards were waiting for them.

"I wish our bank was low like this," said Joe as he leaped from the boat. "We have to go so far downstream before we find a low bank on our side."

"I should think you'd rather walk a mile," said Susie, looking at Joe's shoes, "than come down that bank when it's so muddy."

"Humph! we don't mind a little mud," said Dick, wiping his feet on the grass.

"You've brought some of your land over to us, I see," laughed Uncle Robert. "Mr. Leonard will be obliged to you. He is always glad when the soil is left on his side."

"I don't see why it is," said Joe, "that our land is being cut away all the time and yours is getting bigger. It isn't fair."

"We can't help it, Joe," said Susie. "It's the river that does it. You ask Uncle Robert. He'll tell you all about it."

"I can tell you how it is," said Donald. "You know how strong the current is over on your side? Well, that's the reason your land is washed away. The water flows slower here, so it drops all the stuff it brings with it on our side. See?"

"My!" said Dick, with a mischievous twinkle in his eyes, "doesn't he know a lot!"

"Well, it's so," declared Donald, giving his head a nod. "You can see it yourself if you keep your eyes open."

"My eyes are always open," said Dick, "but that doesn't keep our land."

"You ought to have a creek," said Frank, "if you want your land to grow. Just look, uncle, what a lot of dirt has been left here."

"It makes quite a delta, doesn't it?" replied Uncle Robert.

"Sure enough," said Donald. "You remember the day of our picnic we were going to see if there was one here, and we forgot it."

"Now you see where some of the dirt or silt that is brought down by the creek goes," said Uncle Robert. "And all this must have been left here since the flood in the spring. Frank is right. The creek is really building land all the time."

"Most of the dirt or—what did you call it—silt goes down the river, doesn't it?" asked Frank.

"Our land goes down the river," said Joe; "I've seen it."

"And the river is building land for us," said Donald.

"Yes," said Uncle Robert, "the river works all the time, tearing down in some places and building up in others. The clouds give us rain, the rain goes down into the ground, and then comes out and runs into the streams, and then—"

"Into the ocean," said Frank.

"And then—"

No one spoke.

"And then it rises up from the ocean and comes back again in clouds."

"Did those clouds we had this morning come all the way from the ocean?" asked Joe. "I don't see how they could come so far?"

"The clouds have swift wings to carry them," replied Uncle Robert. "They travel very far without tiring."

"The wind brings the clouds, doesn't it, uncle?" asked Susie.

"Yes, they come on the wings of the wind."

"Oh," said Joe, "I see."

"There's father blowing the horn," said Dick. "We must go."

"Come again," said Uncle Robert and the children together.

"I wish we could hear more about the river," said Joe to Frank as he helped them push off the boat.

"Come over again any day," said Frank. "Uncle Robert will tell you all about it."

"I wish he was my uncle, too," said Dick as they pulled out into the stream. "He isn't a bit stuck up and he knows a lot."

CHAPTER XV.

THE BIG BOOK.

"Please tell us another story from the Big Book," begged Susie as the family were all seated on the piazza one beautiful summer evening.

The great full moon, like a ball of molten iron, was rising in the east. It plowed a silver path across the river. Fireflies glimmered and sparkled in the dusky shadows of the meadow and in and out of the garden shrubs. The merry chirping of the crickets and the low hum of insect voices filled the air. Down by the creek the whip-poor-will told his one story over and over.

"A story from the Big Book!" repeated Uncle Robert. "There are so many and they are all so wonderful. Ever since man was created he has read stories in the earth, water, and sky, and in all living things. Everything he has found in Nature helps him to live and grow wiser and better. We could never understand printed books unless we studied the Big Book. The more we read what God has written the more we shall want to read what other people have found out and put into printed books. The true desire to read these books springs from our love and study of Nature.

"It was written for many years that the sun moved around the earth. But Copernicus studied the sun, earth, and stars anew, and he showed that the printed books were wrong by

143

proving that the earth moved around the sun. Galileo read the same story through the telescope that he made.

"Steam had always been a very common thing. Hot vapor had risen from heated water ever since fire was discovered, but the real story of steam had not been read until Watt sat long hours by a boiling teakettle. Then came the locomotive, the railroad, and mighty engines driving wheels that work for man."

"Wasn't that a good story to read from the Big Book!" said Frank.

"Lightning had flashed and thunder rolled throughout the ages. Men feared, wondered, and worshiped that mighty hidden power. Franklin looked straight at the forked lightning and asked, 'What are you?' The answer came in the telegraph that is fast making the nations of the earth one great family. Bell listened long and carefully to sounds, and now I can talk from New York to my friends in Chicago.

"Are not these stories from the Big Book as wonderful as miracles? These are only a few of the many stories that have been read. Countless more will be read when children really open their eyes to the 'law of the Lord that converteth the soul.' Great men and great minds have road Nature's revelation in the past, but the time is coming when you and I and all children will read every day and hour the hidden things that surround us like light and press upon us like air. The Creator is writing the Big Book all the time for us—His children. Should we not read what He says there?"

The children did not understand all that Uncle Robert said, yet they loved to listen.

"We have found that our farm is a very interesting page of the Book," said Mrs. Leonard.

"Yes, that is the precious thing about it all.

"Whether we look, or whether we listen,
We hear life murmur or see it glisten."

All eyes were gazing at the moon as it seemed to rise above the trees. The great face of the man in the moon became distinct as he looked down upon the rolling earth.

"A beautiful and wonderful world," continued Uncle Robert, "but probably not a bit more wonderful than the countless worlds we see up there.

"Just think! we are on a great round ball, and it is moving on its axis from west to east toward the moon. The moon, you know, does not really move over our heads as it seems to do. The round earth rolls upon its axis, and that makes the moon seem to rise higher and higher, and then sink away below the western horizon."

"To-morrow night it will come up in the east a little later," said Frank.

"Round and round we go upon our ball of earth. The sun seems to rise and set just as the moon does, but it is the world itself that makes the sun and moon seem to rise and set," said Uncle Robert.

"What is our earth made of?" asked Donald.

"Just what you see before you," answered Uncle Robert. "Under our feet we have the ground, the soil, gravel, sand, and loam, which is made of—"

"Ground-up rock," said Frank.

"And underneath the soil there is—"

"The solid rock," said Frank.

"And underneath that?" asked Mr. Leonard.

"We do not know, but it is quite certain the solid earth is made of ground-up rock and rock that may be ground. The mills are all at work, grinding all the time."

GLACIERS ON THE COAST OF NORWAY

"The mills!" said Susie. "Where are the mills?"

"I know one," said Donald. "The river is a great mill. Don't you remember about the pebbles?"

"And the glaciers are mills, too," said Frank.

"Yes, the rivers, the ice rivers or glaciers, the wind, the frost, heat and cold, all grind masses of rock into boulders, pebbles, and sand."

"The rock has been ground so long I should think there would be nothing left but soil," said Frank.

"You saw the limestone down by the spring?" asked Uncle Robert.

"Yes," the children said together.

"That limestone was once soft mud spread out upon the bottom of the ocean in shallow water."

"How do you know that is so, uncle?" questioned Frank.

FOSSIL FISH.

"There are many proofs, but the best proof is that in the limestone are found shells of animals that live in the sea," said Uncle Robert.

"Fossils," said Mrs. Leonard.

"Yes, fossils. They are the remains of plants and animals that lived a very long time ago. Many rocks are almost entirely made of fossils. Fish and shells also have been covered with soft clay and left their imprints. Great beasts have walked in the mud, and we now find their footprints in the hard stone. Coral—you have seen coral?—is often found in limestone. It is made of the shells of little animals, called the polyp, which live in the sea."

"So you see that the firm ground under foot is made of rock, some of which has been ground up over and over again. But there is something else besides rock that makes the world"

"Water," said Donald promptly as he looked down upon the river.

"Yes, the water is just as much a part of our world as the solid rock and the soil. There is water in the soil and in the solid rock, too. It comes out to us in—"

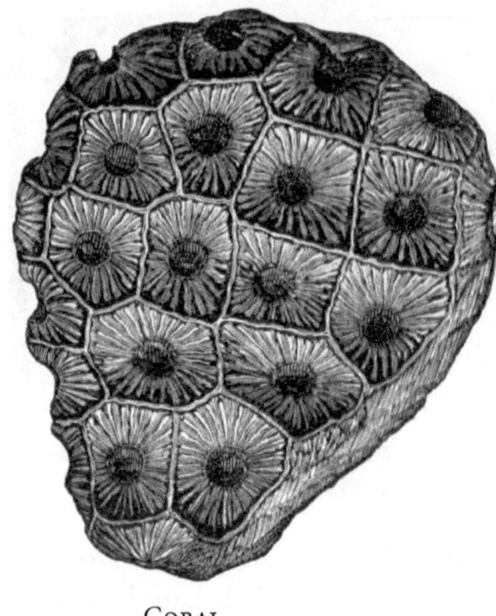

Coral

"Springs," said Donald.

"Water fills hollows in the earth—"

"Ponds and lakes," said Frank.

"Water runs down the slopes—"

"Streams," said Frank.

"Rivers," said Donald.

"There is water in the air—mist, fogs, and clouds— and there is much water in the air which we can not see."

"Vapor?" asked Frank.

"Sometimes water is so thin we can not see it, and again it is so thick and hard that we may walk over it."

"Ice," said Susie.

"Tiny bits of vapor come together until they become so heavy that they fall to the ground."

"Raindrops," said Donald.

"Water is sometimes frozen in the clouds in beautiful white crystals, and then they sail down to the earth."

"Snowflakes," said Susie.

"Sometimes drops start from the clouds and go through very cold air. The cold air freezes them quickly, and then they rattle on the roof and dash on the ground. They cut the corn leaves and destroy the crops."

"Hailstones," said Donald.

"Oh," said Susie, "I saw a hailstone once as big as an egg."

"The lakes are hollows in the ground filled with water. There are many small hollows, and some big ones, but there is one so great that we may call it immense. It is the largest hollow in the world—so large that it occupies three-fourths of the earth's surface."

"The ocean," said Frank.

"Yes, the ocean is only a great big hollow filled with water."

"How deep is the ocean?" asked Frank.

"Very deep in some places—deeper than the height of the highest mountains. In others it is very shallow. In some places bits and masses of land rise out of the ocean."

"Islands?" asked Donald.

"Four great masses of land rise above the ocean level. These immense rock masses are called—"

"Continents," said Frank.

"Yes," said Uncle Robert. "We live on one of them."

"The continent of North America," said Donald.

"Our island rises right out of the river," said Susie.

"Rock and water make only a part of our world. We live on the firm earth. But we live in something. Indeed, we live at the bottom of a great, deep ocean, deeper than the water ocean, and broader than the rock and water surface taken all together."

"We live at the bottom of an ocean!" said Donald in surprise.

"Now you are joking, Uncle Robert," said Susie. "If we lived on the bottom of an ocean we should all drown."

"Fish live in the ocean, and we live in an ocean, too—a very deep one, how deep no one really knows. It may be a hundred, or hundreds of miles deep. We see a part of the surface of the earth and of the water, but no one has ever seen the surface of the mighty ocean in which we live."

Susie and Donald were puzzled. Frank's face lighted up as he said:

"I think you mean the air, Uncle Robert."

"You are right, Frank. The great ocean in which we live is the air, or, as it is called, the atmosphere. The atmosphere is just as much a part of our world as the rock and the water. The rock we may call solid, the water fluid, and the air gaseous. Solid, fluid, gas."

"How do we know that the atmosphere is so deep?" asked Frank.

"We do not know exactly, but there are ways of proving

that it is very, very deep. When people began to study the atmosphere they thought it extended about fifty miles from the surface of the earth. Now they are sure that it is much deeper. We know that air has weight, like soil and water. It presses on us and everything else—"

"Fifteen pounds to the square inch," said Donald.

"We weigh the air with the—"

"Barometer," said Susie.

"It is heavier at the ocean level than it is on the tops of mountains. We are sure that the higher we go up—"

"The less the air weighs," said Frank.

"At the height of fifty miles it is thought to have little or no weight, and so people believed that was as far as it extended. But in time they discovered another way of measuring the atmosphere. You have seen falling stars, haven't you?" asked Uncle Robert.

"Oh, yes," said the three children together.

"I saw a star fall, so fast—just like a rocket. Then the light went out, and I wondered where it went," said Susie.

"Falling stars are not stars at all, though they look like them. They are pieces of rock that break off from other worlds and whiz through space."

"Oh!" said Susie.

"Outside of our atmosphere there may be nothing for these masses of rock

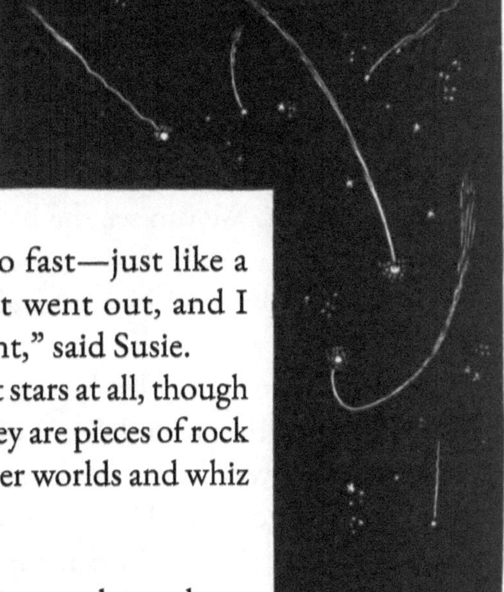

METEORS.

to strike against, but just as soon as they come into the air, it tries to stop them. The air is not strong enough to stop them, but it grinds them up."

"Grinds them up!" exclaimed Donald. "Isn't that wonderful? But, uncle, what makes them look just like fire?"

"If you put an axe or scythe on a dry grindstone and turn the crank, what do you see?"

"Sparks of fire," said Frank.

"Why do you put grease or oil upon the axles of your buggy?"

"To keep them from becoming hot and dry," said Frank. "One time when father and I were on a train there was a hot box, and we had to stop to cool it."

"The heat and the sparks of fire are caused by one body rubbing against another. The faster they move, the greater the heat. This rubbing is called friction."

"There was a time," said Mr. Leonard, "when fires were started by rubbing two pieces of wood together. Some Indians do so now."

"Then the great pieces of rock rub against the air when they whiz through it, and that makes the sparks?" asked Frank.

"You are right. We can see the blaze of fire caused by the friction."

"I should think the rocks would fall on us and kill us," said Donald.

"Most of them are probably ground up into bits of dust before they reach the ground. Some of them, indeed, do strike the ground, and very large ones bury themselves deep in the earth. When we go to the Field Columbian Museum, in Chicago, we shall see these visitors from other worlds. They are called meteoric stones, or meteorites. When they are in the air we call them meteors."

"I am going to watch the next one I see," said Susie.

"They fly so fast that you hardly see them before they are gone," said Donald.

"Men who study the heavens tell of the depth of the atmosphere by the angle the meteor makes in falling, but perhaps you can not understand that now. So you see, children, we live on the bottom of a great ocean of air, and that air, or atmosphere, is a part of our world—the outside part."

"How plain it all is," said Mrs. Leonard, "when we think of it this way!"

"Now we have the land and the water," said Uncle Robert.

"And the atmosphere," put in Donald.

"And they are all right here close to us. Here is the land with its hollows, and there," pointing to the river glistening in the moonlight, "is the water, and—"

"You can't see the air," said Donald.

"We can feel it, anyway," said Susie.

"How large is the earth, uncle?" asked Frank.

"Eight thousand miles through it and twenty-five thousand miles around it," answered Uncle Robert.

"But, uncle, is it all solid rock for eight thousand miles?"

"No one knows. The rocky outside of the ball is called the crust of the earth. Miners have dug down nearly four thousand feet, and makers of artesian wells have bored still farther. They always find rock."

"I wonder how far four thousand feet would be," said Donald.

"A little over three quarters of a mile," said Mr. Leonard.

"The farther they go down into the crust of the earth, the warmer they find it. I have been down in a mine thirty-two

DOWN IN A GOLD MINE

hundred feet, and it was very hot. No one could have lived there if cool air had not been brought down from the surface.

"Some people have thought that inside the crust of the earth the rock is all a molten mass, like melted iron. You have read about volcanoes, and of the lava that is thrown out of them?"

"Does that come out of the inside of the earth?" asked Donald.

"It comes from somewhere in the earth. Some men give their whole lives to the study of these questions, but you know they can not see beneath the crust of the earth. It is thought by some that the weight of the crust would keep the center of the earth a solid mass. So you see there are still many questions unsettled. We know that the crust is moving up and down all the time."

"Oh, I hope the land won't rise here!" said Susie.

"You wouldn't know it, Susie, if it did," said Uncle Robert, laughing.

"Unless there was an earthquake," said Frank.

"Or a volcano," said Donald. "I'd like to see one."

"I would like to see the ocean," said Frank. "It must be grand to stand on the shore and look way off and not see anything but water."

"It is a grand sight, Frank. I have sat on the beach many a time and watched the waves roll in, and thought of the wonderful work the ocean is doing. You know it is the great reservoir that supplies all the land with water."

"The heat of the sun lifts the water up, or evaporates it. The vapor that makes the clouds rises into the air. The winds blow the vapor many long miles, and some of the clouds come right over our heads. The cold air draws the little bits of vapor together and makes the clouds heavy, and down they fall upon the earth as drops of rain.

View of the Ocean

"Some of the rain runs directly into the streams. Some of the rain water sinks down into the earth; in the gravel it sinks fast; in the sand it sinks slower; and in the loam, clay, and rock it sinks very slowly indeed. The water in the ground dissolves the rock or the loose earth into little particles so fine that the tiny roots, or root hairs, drink them up, and so the rock furnishes a part of the nourishment, or food, of plants.

"Without the water that the clouds bring no plant could grow. It gives life and growth to everything that lives, and then sinks deep into the earth. It comes out of the ground again in springs, and flows away in rivulets, brooks, creeks, and rivers— away, and away, back to the ocean again.

"On its way to the ocean it wears down the land, carries silt from place to place, spreads it out on beaches, sand bars, bottom lands, deltas, and on the bottom of shallow places in the ocean."

"Isn't it strange how everything changes, and how all the changes help us?" said Frank thoughtfully.

"Yes, Frank, it is wonderful how the Creator of all things is constantly moving earth, air, and water, and, as you say, making all these changes to help man."

"It is the Big Book that tells us of this marvelous world of ours and of other worlds as well. It lies open before us for us to read every day. God has created and is still creating our home, the dwelling place of His children. We must study Him, my dear children, in all He has made. We must learn of His works in order to use everything to make man happier, better, and more useful."

Mr. Leonard, who had been listening very attentively to the story, said, as his face lighted with a happy smile:

"I never thought of it all in that way before. Every day, in all our work on the farm and in the house—indeed, wherever we may be—we should learn new and beautiful revelations from our Heavenly Father; how much He is constantly giving us, and how thankful we should be."

The moon had risen to its full glory over the earth. The waters of the river glistened. The trees, cornfields, and meadows were peaceful and grand, as though they, too, felt the power of the glorious light.

Susie put her brown arms around her mother's neck and kissed her good-night.

"Oh, how I love the Big Book!" she said.

"I wish I could read it as all those great men have read it," said Frank.

"So do I," said Donald.

"'Day unto day uttereth speech, and night unto night sheweth knowledge,'" mused the mother as her loved ones went to bed with sweet thoughts of a beautiful world and a loving God.